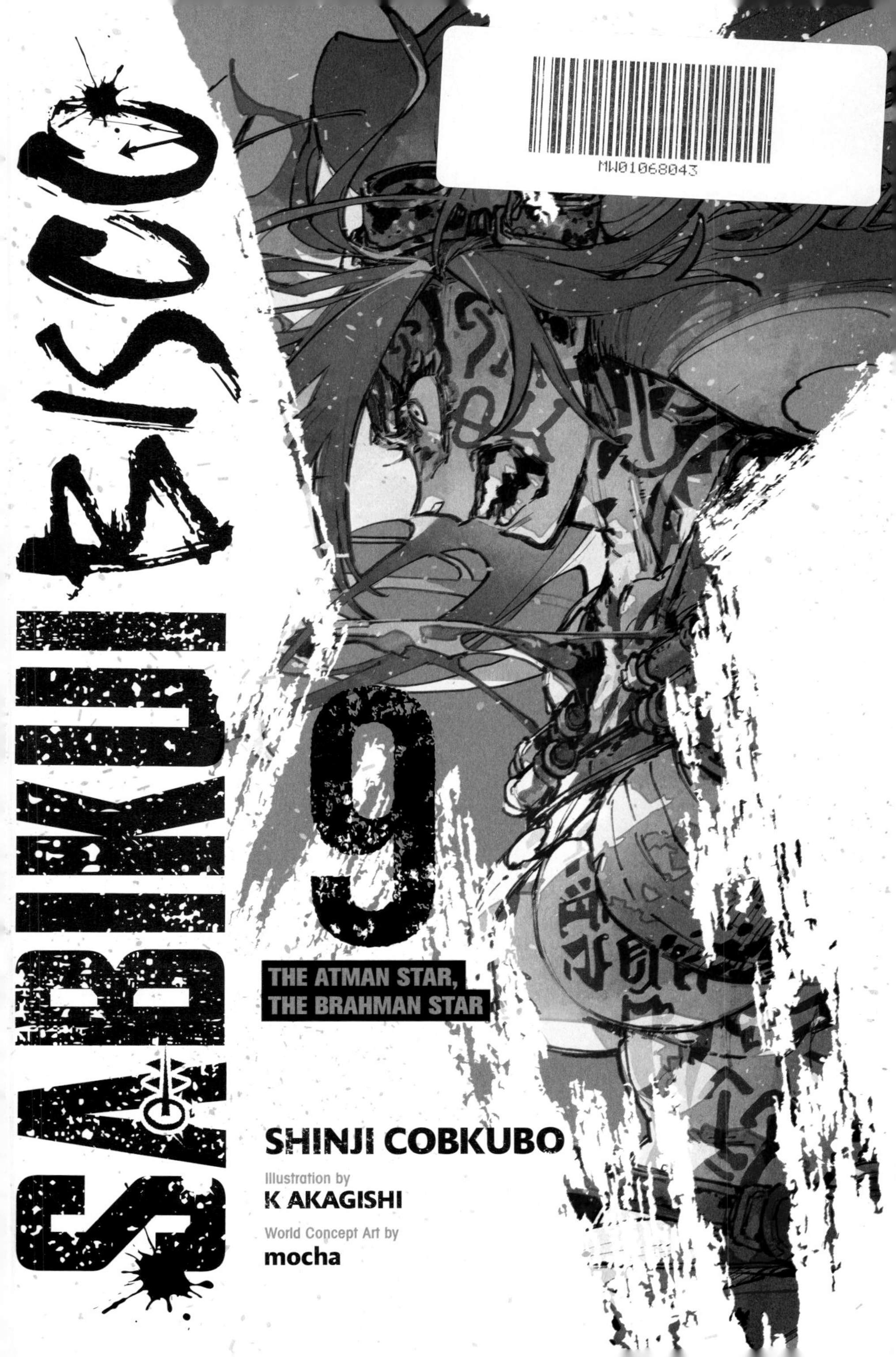
MW01068043
SABIKUI BISCO
9
THE ATMAN STAR,
THE BRAHMAN STAR
SHINJI COBKUBO
Illustration by
K AKAGISHI
World Concept Art by
mocha

SABIKUI BISCO

SHINJI COBKUBO

Illustration by
K AKAGISHI

World Concept Art by
mocha

The Rust Wind eats away at the world. A boy with a bow matches its ferocity.

9

The Atman Star, the Brahman Star

SHINJI COBKUBO

Illustration by
K Akagishi

World Concept Art by
mocha (@mocha708)

SABIKUI BISCO 9

Shinji Cobkubo

Translation by Jake Humphrey

Yen On
150 West 30th Street, 6th Floor
New York, NY 10001

Visit us at yenpress.com † facebook.com/yenpress † twitter.com/yenpress
yenpress.tumblr.com † instagram.com/yenpress

First Yen On Edition: January 2025
Edited by Yen On Editorial: Payton Campbell
Designed by Yen Press Design: Wendy Chan

Yen On is an imprint of Yen Press, LLC.
The Yen On name and logo are trademarks of Yen Press, LLC.

Library of Congress Cataloging-in-Publication Data
Names: Cobkubo, Shinji, author. | Akagishi K, illustrator. | mocha, illustrator. | Humphrey, Jake, translator.
Title: Sabikui bisco / Shinji Cobkubo ; illustration by K Akagishi ; world concept art by mocha ; translation by Jake Humphrey.
Other titles: Sabikui bisco. English
Description: First Yen On edition. | New York, NY : Yen On, 2021- |
Identifiers: LCCN 2021046139 | ISBN 9781975336813 (v. 1 ; trade paperback) | ISBN 9781975336837 (v. 2 ; trade paperback) | ISBN 9781975336851 (v. 3 ; trade paperback) | ISBN 9781975336875 (v. 4 ; trade paperback) | ISBN 9781975336899 (v. 5 ; trade paperback) | ISBN 9781975336912 (v. 6 ; trade paperback)
Subjects: LCGFT: Science fiction.
Classification: LCC PL868.5.O65 S3413 2021 | DDC 895.63/6—dc23/eng/20211001
LC record available at https://lccn.loc.gov/2021046139

ISBNs: 978-1-9753-9892-7 (paperback)
978-1-9753-9893-4 (ebook)

10 9 8 7 6 5 4 3 2 1

LSC-C

Printed in the United States of America

Light-Dark Spacetime Theory

Light-Dark Spacetime Theory, or LDST, is a theory that states the universe is made up of two worlds that exist in harmony, each a mirror reflection of the other.

The theory was first put forward by Densuke Ochagama, the twenty-eighth head priest of Banryouji Temple, and its veracity has yet to be confirmed.

(Source: Encyclopedia Banryoujica)

1

Red stood near the top of Mt. Fuji.

...

A strong night wind blew, caressing her cheeks and fluttering her scarlet hair. She opened her eyes, a jade-green pair brimming with power and determination, and fixed them on the light at the mountain's peak.

Her back, her shoulders, her arms. All were rich in muscle, as hard as rock, and scarred with the records of hundreds of battles. She could splinter a tree just by hugging it.

They called her Twinshroom Red, and she was a Mushroom Keeper, the last of her kind to walk this Earth. She folded her powerful arms and thrust out her intimidating chest.

This is my final fight...
The last stand of Bisco Akaboshi.

Bisco Akaboshi. That was Red's true name. She brought out her arms from beneath her tanshroom cloak and punched her palm, revealing that those arms were covered in crimson tattoos that glistened like hellfire and went all the way up to her collar. Each one of them spoke to her in a language of pain.

You must win, Bisco, they said. *You must succeed where we have failed.*

They were the voices of the dead, bound to Red on her journey. *I will,* she thought back, then traced the line of the tattoos with her finger, covering them once more with her cloak.

Be patient, all of you. Just a little longer now.

The tattoos radiated anger, vengeance, prayers. All of it swirled like a maelstrom inside Red's mind, granting her strength. Every Mushroom Keeper who died before their time was with her.

Failure was not an option. For her sake, for their sakes, and also...

"Bisco!"

A clear voice rang out behind her, and out of the thick forests crawled Red's trusty steed, Actagawa. Atop the crab's back sat Milo Nekoyanagi, otherwise known as Twinshroom Blue.

"I was looking for you! Didn't I tell you it's dangerous to go off by yourself?"

"Milo!"

Milo was Red's partner, and the two were bound on a spiritual level. Milo was a dainty young thing, quite unlike Red at first blush, but the same fire of determination burned in her panda-marked eyes.

"Worried I'd run away?" Red asked.

"Of course not. But I thought you might choose to do this by yourself," said Blue with a sour look.

"I would never. We made a promise, remember?" Red jumped into the saddle beside Blue's and pulled her head into her own breast. "Don't be mad. I told you, when we die, we go together. Got it?"

"Mrh..."

Actagawa fiddled with the ground while the two girls quarreled up top. It was a common sight, including how Blue always seemed to fold in the end to Red's charm.

"...That's not good enough," Blue said at last. "If we die, we have to come back to life. Otherwise, who's going to look after Sugar?"

"Oh yeah, Sugar. How is he?"

"I've put him to sleep in a capsule bed. Tirol set up a mantra barrier, so nobody should be able to hurt him or even know he's there."

"And where'd Tirol get to?"

"Oh."

"Hey, you stupid panda!"

An educated-sounding voice rang out after the pair, followed by incessant panting as a short jellyfish-haired young boy emerged from the forest.

"What's the big idea? Don't just leave me alone while I'm putting up a barrier!"

"I-I'm sorry! I just got worried about Bisco, and—"

"Get on, Tirol!"

Red smiled and offered her arm, while the sweat-drenched young lad by the name of Tirol shot her a deadly glare over the rim of his black-framed glasses, which had slipped down his nose.

After a short while, he pushed them up, snorted derisively, then accepted Red's help and climbed atop Actagawa's back, where he sat among the saddlebags.

"Remember, Akaboshi," he said. "You'll only have one chance to stop the Rust god."

The name Tirol spoke was that of the Mushroom Keepers' deadly foe. The Rust god sought to enslave humanity and reign eternal in the silence of destruction. Red, Blue, Tirol, and Actagawa were the only ones left who could stand against him. Their mission was to destroy the Rust god and put a stop to his machinations once and for all.

"With those hawklike eyes of yours, you should be able to fire off a shot before the god notices you. Just remember that even Pawoo couldn't bring him down with his staff. If you catch his attention, you won't get a second chance."

"..."

Blue cast her eyes downward, and her long eyelashes quivered. Red felt the tattoos across her skin burn hotter than ever.

"...I'll beat that thing. Pawoo's sacrifice won't be in vain."

"Bisco..."

"Let's go."

With conviction in her heart, Red took up her bow.

"The power of all those we've lost lies inside me," she said. "So believe in me, Milo. We'll all win this and come back, and hold Sugar in our arms again."

Blue paused, looked up into her sparkling jade eyes, and nodded.

"Yeah!"

Then she took up Actagawa's reins and began steering her to the peak of the mountain. Red looked out over the ruined world below, and as the wind caressed her crimson hair, the souls inside her made their voices heard.

Kill him, Bisco. Kill the Rust god.

Even if it breaks your bones or burns your flesh.

I will!

In response to the spirits' urging, her jade-green eyes sparkled with determination.

I won't fail you, I swear!

You all died for me. I have to return the favor!

2

"Aaaaagh I won't lose!!"

Bisco sat up in bed, yelling.

He was inside a large tent. A single lantern hung from the ceiling, illuminating the sleeping forms of his family. Bisco tried to remember just what he was shouting about, but…

"…???"

…a whirlwind of fiery emotions took control of his sleep-addled mind.

…What am I doing sleeping? Why am I here? I was just on Mt. Fuji with Milo, and then…

Bisco looked down at himself, but the flesh-searing tattoos were gone. Without them, he felt naked and cold. He folded his arms across himself and shivered.

"Papa?"

Just then, he heard a sleepy voice and turned to see Sugar sitting up beside him, rubbing her eyes.

"What's wrong, Papa?"

"Sugar…"

Bisco looked at his daughter and froze for a while. The gears turned, and then suddenly he jumped and held her tight.

"Sugar! Wh-what happened to your barrier?!"

"Barrier??"

"We have to put you back, or you'll be in danger! I remember now! The Rust god is gonna—"

"Rust god?"

"...???"

Who on earth was that? Bisco didn't recognize the name, even though it had come from his own mouth. He just sat there, lips flapping wordlessly, until Sugar slapped her father's cheeks and spoke to him in a tired yet scolding tone.

"It was probably just a nightmare, Papa," she said. "Don't be scared; Sugar's here to protect you!"

"Uh...no...but..."

"We're gonna play at the beach all day tomorrow, so you gotta have your sleep. Go to beddy-byes now, Papa."

"No, wait, listen to me!"

"No. Nighty-night."

Then Sugar collapsed into bed once more and began snoring immediately. Bisco stared at her for a few moments, dumbfounded.

Sugar and Milo were sleeping on his right.

Pawoo and Salt were sleeping on his left.

Also, Tirol was there, for some reason, and Bisco could still sense the presence of his trusty steed, Actagawa, right outside the tent. It was just another night in their ordinary life of travels. Bisco's memories slowly started coming back to him, replacing the events of the bizarre dream in his mind.

What...did I see?

I don't remember anymore.

All I remember...is how it felt.

Felt like a bad fuckin' omen.

Hope it don't come true.

Better pay my respects at the next clan remembrance service...

* * *

Bisco laid his head down on the pillow next to his daughter's, but his mind was reeling with the implications of what he had seen.

I can't sleep!

And so the night passed without Bisco knowing another dream.

SHINJI COBKUBO

Illustration by **K Akagishi**

World Concept Art by **mocha (@mocha708)**

The Atman Star, the Brahman Star

3

Atop Mt. Fuji, a lone young man sat on a throne carved into the very rock. He sat crossed-legged, chin in hand, staring into space without love or care. The wind caressed his face, but the boy didn't so much as blink, and around his head swirled countless balls of light—human souls.

Grant our prayers.
Grant our prayers.
O Lord Rust, O Lord Rust...

Each one gave off only a faint glow, but they swarmed the boy's head in such great numbers that they made the peak of Mt. Fuji shine as bright as day.

Grant our prayers.
Riches.
Wisdom.
Power.
Grant our prayers. Grant our prayers.

The young boy, Lord Rust, simply sighed. Without lifting his head, he raised one hand and snapped his fingers.

* * *

Oh!
Gold! Gold!
Wealth beyond measure!
Ohhh!

About a third of the whirling souls shone brighter and trembled with sublime joy. In death's last pantomime, their wishes were granted, and afterward, they were drawn in and absorbed by the strange young boy.

Ohhh, me too.
Me too.
Grant our prayers. Grant our prayers.

"..."

The boy let out another sigh and snapped his fingers again and again. Each time, another fraction of the lost souls had their wishes granted and glowed with joy.

Ohhh, so wise I am!
No one is mightier than I!
So happy! So happy!

With their hearts' desires realized, albeit only in the endless dream of death, the souls swore fealty to the Rust god and became a part of him. Before Lord Rust had even snapped his fingers ten times, there were no souls remaining. After finishing his meal—the same as the last and all before it—Lord Rust let out a little burp.

"...Urp."

But far from being pleased that his stomach was filled, Rust felt only disgust for the souls he had consumed, and his expression did not change in the slightest, as though something was bugging him.

All of a sudden, a fly flew out from behind his ear.

"Lord Rust. Lord Rust."

It circled his head a few times before landing on his shoulder.

"How was your feast, my lord? I, your humble servant, N'nabadu, did most assuredly tire and toil to bring you only the most succulent—"

"Repulsive."

Rust did not even glance in the fly's direction.

"It was like drinking fetid mud," he said. "All were vulgar souls, with not a single desire of substance to be found."

"I am most sorry they were not to your liking, my lord. I will endeavor to—"

"It is your buzzing that is not to my liking, fly. Begone at once."

"Ohhh, forgive me, Lord Rust!" N'nabadu suddenly began flying in a panic, finally landing on the boy's smooth hand and kissing the back of it over and over again. *"I promise you I will do it right next time, so please forgive me, Lord Rust! I cannot go on without your benevolence! I need you!"*

"And yet I do not need you, fly."

"Pray, do not say such hurtful things, my lord!"

N'nabadu smiled and danced in an attempt to improve the Rust god's mood. He was only a few centimeters long, but he wore a solid gold collar and golden rings that dazzled the eyes as he flew.

Hmph...

Lord Rust didn't even seem annoyed by the fly's sycophantic antics. He just gave another deep sigh. Though the god's glacial expression had not budged, N'nabadu was wise to the imperceptible alterations in his master's temperament. And so, sensing his mood had mellowed, the fly took off once more, buzzing.

"If your meal has settled, my lord, then it is time to get off that throne and do some exercise. A walk will do you a world of good."

"Hmm."

At the fly's suggestion, Rust stood up. The divine being was not of flesh and blood, as the cogwheels decorating his body attested. He was an automaton without a power source, like the protagonist of some futuristic manga series.

"Ahh, you walk like an angel, my dear Lord Rust. This way, if you please. See? Gaze upon the world below. Do you see those figures of rust over there?"

"I do."

"Those are the hollow shells of those who were awed by your magnificence and came to offer their souls."

They littered the mountainside like statues, completely devoid of life. The boundless vitality of humankind, reduced to nothing before the miracles of a god.

"We don't even need to kill them to obtain their souls these days. It makes things much easier for us."

"...Why did they not simply try to kill me?" asked Lord Rust, gazing upon the rows of statues with scorn. "If they had combined their forces, it might have been possible. Instead, they chose servitude."

"Why, that's because you make their dreams come true, my lord! All for the low, low price of their immortal souls!"

N'nabadu gesticulated wildly as he spoke.

"They'd never get that kind of satisfaction here on Earth, that's for sure! And you get to eat your fill! It's a win-win! A win-win-win, even!"

"..."

Back when the Rust god had first descended to this world, he had acquired his souls in honorable combat. But as his power and influence grew, mankind gradually gave up hope, and it was then that N'nabadu came up with a crafty idea.

"Offer your soul freely, and your wish will be granted."

This notion spread through the human folk like wildfire, until only a handful of people remained who would stand against the Rust god of their own volition.

"Just look at these analytics, my lord!"

The fly buzzed this way and that, tracing a graph of the god's conquest in the air.

"Two hundred sixty million souls in this month alone! By now, ninety-nine percent of male humans and ninety-eight percent of females have..."

Rust didn't so much as look in N'nabadu's direction. His cold gaze was fixed unerringly on the statues—all that remained of the humans who had given their lives.

"I have granted no wishes," he said. "All I have done is offered comforting dreams."

"What is wrong with that, my lord? It brings you more souls than ever before!"

"All of them utterly tasteless," Rust replied, thinking back to the early days of his conquest. "The greatest souls belonged to those brave warriors that refused to surrender. No meal is as sublime as the one that is earned through merciless subjugation."

Rust had a nose for quality—the kind of sadistic quality few people could understand. N'nabadu, with his head for figures, was not one of them.

"There you go again, my lord. You really must get with the times."

"Or perhaps it is you."

"Hyuk!"

"Perhaps *you* are doing something to my souls, degrading them..."

"L-Lord Rust, please calm..."

"Repulsive insect."

All of a sudden, Rust's eyes lit up, and two thermonuclear beams shot from his face, sizzled the wings of the hapless fly, and continued to a distant hill, setting the wildlife there alight.

"M-my lord! Have mercy!!"

"I wish to devour a great soul. One with fire, defiance, and grit."

Rust's heart was far more set on this than N'nabadu had envisioned. But the heroes of men had dwindled, and precious few remained with the courage to stand against him.

"...Of course."

It was then that Rust had an idea.

"The Mushroom Keepers. One yet lives, does she not?"

At these unexpected words, N'nabadu froze, startled.

"L-Lord Rust... What did you say?"

"The Mushroom Keepers were a proud people who never bent to my rule. I believe one still remains. Her name is Red the Twinshroom."

"R-Red the Twinshroom?"

N'nabadu leaped up at the mention of that unspeakable name. As loudly as he could, he buzzed his objections.

"Y-you cannot, my lord! You mustn't concern yourself with the foul soul of a Mushroom Keeper!"

The Mushroom Keepers had been the greatest obstacle to Rust's initial conquest, and N'nabadu still harbored disdain for their kind.

"It troubles me to think of even one of those barbarians becoming part of your majesty! Listen well, my lord. Those Mushroom Keepers are nothing but rebels who begrudge us our peaceful ruin! They want the world to remain harsh and unforgiving! They're just a bunch of miserable, self-destructive...assholes!"

"Watch your tongue, fly."

"Oh, terribly sorry, Lord Rust! Oh-ho-ho-ho... Grr... I would sooner be rid of their kind, but the problem is that soul-absorbing sorcery they possess!"

N'nabadu thought of Red and ground his teeth.

"It allows the Mushroom Keepers to absorb the souls of the fallen, in a way not dissimilar to your own ability, my lord. Red now possesses over a thousand of her allies, painted onto her skin as those vile tattoos..."

"Hmm. Interesting..."

"No, not interesting at all! Stay away, I beg you!"

The fly let out a frustrated squeal, tearing at his handkerchief.

"I will take care of the Twinshrooms, Red and Blue, my lord. Do you understand? Do not concern yourself with those two humbugs!"

"Humbugs...?"

The irony of the fly's wording was not lost on the young god, but even that failed to elicit so much as a chuckle. N'nabadu fiddled with a device in his hand that projected a list of names into the air.

"Forget all about Red, my lord. There are plenty of far greater souls on this list; just take your pick. What are you in the mood for tonight...?"

Tiring of the fly's antics, Lord Rust shifted his gaze to the moon above—a full moon that shone like the sun. He stared at it, allowing the silver light to envelop his soft features.

...Hmm?

A black spot. Rust noticed a small shadow framed against the celestial sphere.

What is that? he thought. *It looks almost like a large...crab?*

As soon as he recognized the shape, Lord Rust felt the intensity of its will, and his hair bristled. It was coming for him; he could feel it!

"That's enough, fly," he said.

"Enough? What do you mean?"

"It seems she has decided to come to me instead."

"She? Who is—?"

Fwoosh!

Rust grabbed N'nabadu in his fist and sprang aside, mere moments before the distant speck unleashed an arrow, like lightning, which blazed across the sky and embedded itself in Mt. Fuji's summit!

Gaboom!!

"Aaaaaghh?!?!"

A mushroom explosion! A bright-red toadstool burst out of the earth, followed by another and another. Lord Rust dodged the first two, but the third finally caught him and flung him high into the air.

"Oh."

"Such power! This can only be the work of one woman!!"

"So, you've come, Twinshroom Red."

A tiny, almost imperceptible passion worked its way into Rust's emotionless facade.

"Look at this, she's left a hole in the side of Mt. Fuji."

"This isn't the time to be impressed! You've got to get away, Lord Rust!"

"I'm trying to. However..."

Rust stared at his fingertips, but they wouldn't move at all. The toadstool's terrifying poison had already worked its magic.

"...I appear to be paralyzed."

"Wh-what?!"

Rust sailed through the air, helpless, all the while failing to give the matter the gravity it deserved. He watched as, from the direction of the full moon, a second arrow fast approached!

"At last," he said. "A worthy foe."

"L-Lord Rust!!!"

Thud!!

* * *

Gaboom! Gaboom!

Gaboom!!

"Got him!!"

Red sat atop Actagawa's back, drenched in sweat. The sheer concentration was causing her tattoos to give off an immense heat. Blue guided Actagawa to land, and the four of them stood in the light of the glowing mushrooms.

"Did you see that, Milo?" said Red. "A direct hit, right in the kisser! We showed that Rust god what's what!"

"Don't celebrate just yet! The arrow was so strong, we're going to get caught up in it, too!"

"All right, Actagawa, get us outta here!"

The giant crab followed the directions of her mistress at the reins, leaping back from the approaching toadstool swarm, just seconds before it obliterated any and all trace of the Rust god's throne atop the summit of Mt. Fuji.

The wind coursed through Red's crimson hair. "We managed to beat it!!" she cried, overcome with relief. "Pawoo, Jabi… Did you see that? Our arrow took that thing down!"

Blue finally took her cautious eyes off the situation to look across at her partner. "Bisco…," she muttered. "Now that the Rust god's dead, we can finally set all those souls free."

Red looked ready to cry. "…Yeah!"

"We worked so hard for this, Bisco. You most of all! I mean, look at that toadstool! I've never seen one so big! Some parts got blasted all the way over—"

But Milo didn't get any further than that. For she saw something that made her tug on Actagawa's reins!

…?!?!

The bits and bolts of Lord Rust's body, scattered by the blast, suddenly began to coalesce.

"Milo?!"

"Bisco!! It…it's not over yet!"

All of a sudden, the upper torso of the Rust god reappeared in midair, giving a whirling right hook to Actagawa's flank! Actagawa was sent hurtling back, and Lord Rust ignited a pair of rocket boosters at his waist, speeding after her.

"It's nice to finally meet you, Red."

"What?! We killed you!!"

"I am a god. I am…Rust."

Then the Rust god unleashed another punch. Red summoned the full strength of her rippling muscles and crossed her arms to block, but…

"Hrgh?! Whoa!!"

Despite the nearly twofold discrepancy in their physiques, the force of Rust's blow flung Red from the saddle and tossed her across the landscape like an empty tin can. There was unthinkable power behind the god's slender frame.

"Bisco!!" Blue yelled, drawing her shortsword and rushing at Rust from behind, but…

"Hmph."

"Waaaagh!!"

Again, with unimaginable strength, Rust effortlessly blocked the blow and sent Blue flying back. This time, it was with a pair of legs that swiftly materialized and delivered a devastating spinning kick. Both girls rolled across the mountainside before finally landing in a cloud of dust and smoke.

"Milo!!"

"Urgh…"

"Dammit… Dammit!"

Bleeding profusely, Red dragged herself over to Blue and lifted the girl in her arms. The fire in her eyes was now tempered with an equal measure of shock.

"I thought…I killed you!!" she growled.

"You did."

Rust rejoined his upper and lower halves, before calmly walking toward Red. He rotated his hips, testing the connection, his face as cold as ice throughout.

"I commend you on your flawless technique," he said. "However, killing me once or twice is not enough."

"Wh-what…do you mean?!"

"I am a god. I have as many lives as the souls I have swallowed."

This revelation struck Red dumb. No matter how powerful a human, one death brought their tale to a close. To Lord Rust, however, a death sentence was nothing more than a flesh wound.

"Why are you lying in the dirt?" he asked. "Rise. We must continue our battle."

"Wh-what?!"

"I like people like you. People with strength. Proud warriors who cast off the fetters of their fate and carve out their own lives. Do you know why?"

Just then, a horrifying grin spread across Rust's lips.

"Because nothing gives me more joy than seeing those warriors broken at my feet, begging for mercy! And the greater the soul, the greater the satisfaction!"

"Y-you psycho!!"

The young boy was only a disguise. In truth, Lord Rust was nothing but a raging sadist. The enemy of all life on Earth.

"You're an insult to all brave warriors of this land!!" Red yelled.

"Including you, don't forget. Soon, you will weep like the rest of them wept!"

"Never!!"

Just then, Red spotted a cloud of dust over Rust's shoulder. It was her giant crab ally, shell cracked from the god's attack, racing to her rescue.

"Actagawa!"

"You still don't seem to understand me, Red," said Rust, arms folded, not even deigning to glance in the crab's direction. "How can I make you put your all into this fight? ...Hmm, I know."

Rust suddenly spun around, staring right at the approaching crab.

"What if it is to avenge the death of a sworn sister?"

Behind the windows of the god's eyes, cogwheels churned into motion, and the gears furnishing Rust's wrists began to spin, generating unfathomable amounts of energy.

"Stop!!" screamed Red. "Actagawa! Get out of the way!!"

However, her desperate pleas fell on deaf ears. Actagawa was dead set on protecting her mistress's life. The giant crab raised her greatclaw, ready to bring it down on the Rust god's head!

"Don't look away, Red," said Rust. "This happened because you are weak."

"No!!"

"Die."

Red watched as Rust drove his fist through the crab's underbelly. Witnessing the death of her bonded companion, she let out a soul-rending scream.

"Nooooo!! Actagawaaaaaa!!"

4

"Actagawaaaaa!!"

Bisco bolted upright and scanned his surroundings, face dripping with sweat. His heart was pounding so hard, he could feel it in his throat, and there was a pain deep in his soul, like somebody had torn out half of his heart. A vision of death remained seared into his mind, but right now that scene was nowhere to be seen.

Where did Rust go?! Wait… Who's Rust?

All Bisco found was the pleasant summer wind and the emerald sea stretched out before him.

…It happened again. Another weird-ass dream!!

Starved of sleep from the previous night, Bisco had fallen asleep on the beach. He tried to cast his mind back to his dream, but he couldn't remember a thing about it.

Actagawa was nearby, sitting in the shade of a large palm tree, nibbling on a coconut. He looked up at Bisco with a displeased expression, as if to say, *"What's all this fuss about? You're disturbing my rest."*

"…A…A…Actagawaaa!!"

The giant crab was stoic in the face of most things, but even he was forced to reel in shock at the sight of his sworn younger brother bounding over with an eager embrace. The force shook the palm tree, which dislodged a coconut, which fell right between Actagawa's eyes. But just as the crab was about to yell, *"What's the big idea?!"* or some approximation thereof…

"Actagawa… Thank the gods you're okay…!!"

Looking at his brother's weeping form, Actagawa felt his confusion win out over his anger. He made no attempt to break the embrace, but instead softly and awkwardly patted Bisco's back with his smaller claw.

* * *

"Don't that just mean you've been seein' into the dark world?"

"The dark world???"

"Yeah, it's like the mirror opposite of our light world," the swimsuit-clad Tirol explained, leaning back in her beach chair made of mushrooms. With a pink tropical drink in one hand, she elegantly uncrossed and recrossed her legs. "Grandpappy came up with this theory, see, that our world is one of two in a helical configuration. The dark world is basically a reflection of ours, mostly similar but with minor differences."

"Huh…"

Tirol suggested it almost as a prank, and she was hoping for a funny reaction from Bisco, but seeing him instead grow sullen and contemplative, she raised her sunglasses and sat up straight.

"Hey, don't take it too seriously," she said. "It's just a dream. Did it really feel that real?"

"Well, this ain't the first time it's happened, either," Bisco replied. "You see, I was a woman, and…"

"You?! A woman?!!"

"You were there, too," Bisco went on. "As a guy."

"Me on a gender bender, huh? Hard to imagine, really…"

"And the world…humans had all had their souls absorbed by this dude, the Rust god. We were tryin' to bring 'em all back—me and Milo were—and then…"

Tirol wasn't sure what to do with the unusually meek Bisco. She gave him a few hearty slaps on the back and chuckled.

"Well, there's no use worryin' about it!" she said. "Even if that was a glimpse into an alternate reality, the theory says the two worlds can never interact, so there ain't diddly-squat you can do about it! Just be glad we were all born into the *good* timeline, eh, Akaboshi?"

"Hmm..."

"Papa!!"

A voice out in the sea drew the pair's attention.

"Look at me, Papa! I'm surfing!"

Bathed in the sun's rays, Sugar stood atop a board made of spores, riding the waves with expert precision...or so it seemed at first glance. Upon closer examination, her poise was owing to a group of monstroom folk, clutching the board from below and frantically treading water with their stubby legs.

"Glub! Glub!"

"Seawater's salty!"

"You don't have a mouth."

"Oh yeah..."

"Get ready, all of you! There's another wave on its way!"

""""Bab-ba-ba-bam!""""

They, like Sugar, were enjoying their first foray into the ocean. Most people avoided the dangerous waters around Japan and would never enter without a full set of body armor, let alone in a bikini. But Sugar's boyfriend-in-a-bottle Mare was a god of the sea, and having him on her side kept the predators well away.

And so Tirol's clever suggestion was that they capitalize on this fact and conduct an Akaboshi family outing.

"Sugar!" Bisco yelled. "Cover up! What did I say about puttin' on your bathing suit?"

"Why don't ya take a dip, too, Akaboshi?" suggested Tirol. "Everybody dreams of goin' into the ocean these days."

"Sure, I will. Later."

"Whaddaya mean, 'later'?! You're missin' your one and only chance to swim with your daughter! And you've still got all your clothes on! Are you goin' in or not?!"

"Urgh…!!"

Bisco Akaboshi was scared. The ocean's depths terrified him, and he chomped his nails whenever he thought of what lurked there. He was even still wearing his stuffy Mushroom Keeper garb, right down to the cloak.

"I will!" he yelled. "It's just…I gotta mentally prepare myself. Gimme two more hours."

"What are you so afraid of?! You've been in the water before, ain't ya?"

Bisco thought back to his previous underwater adventure with Milo and Actagawa. "I was young and reckless back then!" he protested. "I didn't know! The souls of the restless dead gather down there in the ocean trenches—Milo said so!"

"He's just messin' with ya! He knows you're a fraidy-cat, that's why—"

"And another thing: Jabi's watchin' over me, but the old man couldn't swim for shit! How's he supposed to look after me if I go down there?!"

He's hopeless!

Bisco had taken Milo's ghost stories at face value, and even here in broad daylight, he feared the specters' wrath. Meanwhile, as her father chattered his teeth in fright, Sugar drifted farther and farther out to sea.

"See that, Akaboshi?! Your daughter's leavin' you behind!"

"Wait, no!"

"You'll miss your chance at this rate. Ain't you gonna regret that for the rest of your life?"

"Sugar! Wait!"

"You gotta do more than just shout, Akaboshi! What are you, a sea urchin?"

"Grh!"

The resemblance was uncanny. Tirol slapped him on the back, causing Bisco to stagger forward and lock eyes on his daughter, who even now continued drifting away, amid the dazzlingly clear sea and blinding sun.

"Yoo-hoo!!" she yelled. "Hello, everyone!!"

When the young girl waved, a sea turtle lazily turned to look at her, and small fish leaped out of the ocean. A large shadow in the water beneath her spouted water, tossing her giggling form high into the air.

"Whee! Ha-ha-ha!"

The sea welcomed their divine neighbor with open arms. Sugar keenly felt the beat of the land, alive thanks to the great deeds of her mother and father, and all the many heroes who had come before them. None of this would have existed without every last one of them.

This is Earth, she thought. *My planet!*

Boundless love filled the young girl's heart, and she felt determined to protect all life within her motherly embrace, now and forever.

It was at that moment of sublime clarity that something astonishing happened.

"Guh."

"Eek?!"

Sugar was dazzled by a blinding flash of light, and all of a sudden, something orange like the sun came out of the sky, blazing over the sea like a falling star.

What's that?!

A single falling star was not too much cause for alarm, but the worrying thing about this one was that it seemed to be falling straight toward Sugar.

"Whaaat?!" cried the monstrooms. "The sky's falling!" "Run away!"

Their terror was unsurprising, for the approaching meteor gave off such heat that even the sea beneath started to boil up and evaporate away.

The monstrooms all looked to their leader for advice, but…

"Oh no, she's got that look!"

"You're gonna fight it?"

"Of course!" beamed the young girl with pride. "If I don't save the Earth, who will?!"

What manner of foe stood in the Akaboshis' way this fateful day? Sugar didn't know yet, but it didn't change what she had to do. She raised her arm, flashed her father's signature canine-baring grin, and called out to the monstrooms.

"Come on, you lot! You know the drill!"

""""Aww…""""

"No whining! Just do it!"

""""Bab-ba-ba-bam!""""

The monstrooms instantly vaporized into a cloud of spores, then swirled and re-formed in Sugar's open hand. The rainbow shimmer slowly took form, and then…

"Come to me, Mushy Magic Pole!!"

Swish! Swish! Swish! Fwip!

With her divine weapon by her side, Sugar ascended into the sky like a lightning bolt in reverse. She swung her staff, leaving a rainbow trail.

"How's this for a home run?!"

Her swing struck the meteor head-on!

Clangg!!

"Wah! It's so hard!!"

The meteor was far heavier than Sugar had expected, but her hit was clean, and she still managed to swat the object back, which left a rainbow arc as it fell into the sea.

That wasn't any ordinary meteor.

Sugar felt a strange power lurking within the object. Strike first, before the threat becomes a threat—that was the Mushroom Keeper way, passed down by Bisco, and Jabi before him. Sugar raised her staff once more, kicked off the surface of the water, and prepared to obliterate the smoking object with a downward swing.

"Hi-yaaaaaa—!!"

"…Ugh…"

"—ah?!!"

The meteor groaned! At the last minute, Sugar swerved her aim, striking the surface of the sea with an enormous splash. Leaving it bobbing in the water, she took a closer look at the object itself.

I…it's…

As the water cooled the object and its glow faded, Sugar saw…

It's a person!!

Quite a largely built person, at that. Their muscles were like rock and inhumanly hard, which explained why they were so easily mistaken for a meteor. But there was something even more surprising about them.

It's…a woman!

Not only that, but the figure was completely naked. Sugar's face lit up like a traffic light, and she panicked, trying to avert her eyes.

Wh-why isn't she wearing any clothes?!?!

"Is…is someone there…?" the glowing human asked. Sugar froze in fright, and the mysterious woman groaned again. "Milo…huh? I'm glad…you're okay. I'll protect you…don't worry…"

"Um! Don't try to move, lady! You're in the sea!"

"Shit…my eyes are burnt…I can't see…your face…"

"Just hang on! Hup!"

Sugar conjured a mushroom to stand on, and then…

"Up we go…"

…with great effort, she dragged the woman up onto it. Looking at her face, Sugar saw that her eyeballs had melted—they had probably burned up along with her clothes when she fell from the sky.

It made for a tragic sight, but…

…This lady's not an ordinary person. She's like a god!

Immediately, Sugar felt the immense latent power dwelling inside the woman's tattoos. She couldn't tell whether the power was from prayers or curses, but it was certainly of human origin.

In any case, regenerating her eyes would be child's play.

"You'll be okay, lady! You're in Sugar's hands now!"

"Sugar…you say??"

Following the goodness of her heart, Sugar summoned up her Ultra-faith power. She gripped the woman's chin and made her look up, before gathering the miracle rainbow spores in her fingertips.

"I'll give you some clothes, too!"

"…Who…are…?"

Sugar traced her fingers along the woman's face, and the rainbow spores got to work, re-creating her beautiful jade-green eyes. After that, they enwreathed her body, bestowing her with a full set of Mushroom Keeper garb.

"Ta-daa!" said Sugar when it was done. "It's a mushroom miracle! You're welcome!"

"..."

"It's a good thing Sugar was nearby," Sugar went on. "You've got good sense, lady. If you'd have fallen anywhere else, you'd be—"

"Sugar."

"Hwah?!"

"Sugar!"

Squeeze!

The woman suddenly wrapped her big, strong arms around Sugar and pulled her into a gentle yet firm embrace. With her head sandwiched between the woman's breasts, Sugar went bright red, struggling for breath as her mouth flapped wordlessly.

"Ha...hawawa?!?!"

"I missed you so much...!!"

Her voice cracked. Her emotions overflowed. Meanwhile, caught in the woman's grasp, Sugar spouted spores like a teakettle, her eyes as wide as dinner plates.

You've mistaken me for someone else! she wanted to scream, but unfortunately, her mouth was not free to speak. Of course, the little god could have fought her way out of the grapple easily, but she didn't. Because...

Sh-she's crying?!

...the woman was shaking even harder than she was.

"I'm sorry! I'm so, so sorry! I'll never leave you alone again! We'll always be together...!!"

...

"...Wait a minute. Sugar's a boy!"

All of a sudden, like a bolt from the blue, the mysterious woman seemed to realize something.

"This isn't my world?!"

"Wahhh!!" cried Sugar as the woman tossed her aside and began madly scanning her surroundings. Sugar had more than a few complaints about the way she was being treated, but she opted not to voice them, for the woman clearly had enough troubles as it was.

"The sky's blue. The wind is clear. This isn't the dark world at all! This is the light world! Another timeline! I didn't think it really existed!"

"L-light world...??"

"Tirol must have sent me here," the woman went on. "Which means... we failed? Dammit, my memory's foggy, I can't remember a thing!"

The woman tore at her hair, desperately trying to recall. Watching her slow descent from a loving goddess into a crazed maniac, Sugar began to tremble.

"...But I do remember one thing," the woman said at last. "I remember my mission!"

Her eyes lit up with flames of determination, and the tattoos all over her body burst to life.

Eat, Bisco.
Devour your other self...

"If this really is a mirror world, then there's gotta be a reflection of me here, too! I got to find 'em, and..."

"Waaaaaargh!! Sugaaar!!"

"Papa!"

Just as Sugar was wondering what to do with the strange woman, a helping hand emerged in the form of an orange shell blazing its way across the sea. After seeing the meteor come for his daughter, it seemed that Bisco had finally overcome his fear of the ocean and was on his way, atop Actagawa's back.

"Papa!" Sugar shouted with a wave and a smile. "Over here!"

"Sugar!! Get away from there!" Bisco yelled back.

"Oh?" Sugar suddenly dropped her hand and looked puzzled, while the woman turned her curious eyes on Bisco.

"Who's this street punk...?" she wondered aloud. Then two pairs of identical jade-green eyes met. The largely built woman's and Bisco's.

"""!!"""

Something stirred in their very souls. A recognition and primal hate that moved far faster than word or thought. Neither of them knew why, but they were both thinking the exact same thing.

"I don't know who you are, but I can't let you beat me!"

"Hide behind me, Sugar!"

It was the woman who moved first. She grabbed Sugar and leaped backward, cloak aflutter. Bisco watched, agog, as the woman brazenly kidnapped his daughter.

"Hey!! That's my kid! Whaddaya think you're doing?! Let her go!!"

Bisco swiftly unhooked his bow and drew an arrow. The point glowed with the light of the Rust-Eater, and then Bisco unleashed a sunlight-colored streak toward the mysterious woman.

There was nothing on this Earth capable of stopping Bisco's arrow, once loosed. But the woman was not of this Earth.

"You think that's enough to stop me, you damn fake?!"

She brought up her cloak like a shield! Upon impact, the arrow's momentum was completely drained, causing it to hang in midair. Even Sugar was stunned by this incredible display of control.

"Sugar Akaboshi..."

"What?! My arrow?!"

"...is my kid!!"

The woman plucked the arrow out of the air and, calling upon the incredible force of her muscles, *threw* it back toward Bisco. The ocean rose, parted by the shock, and the arrow hurtled toward Bisco, no slower than when it was fired from his bow.

"Aaargh! Actagawa!!"

He tugged on the reins, and the giant crab raised his greatclaw, knocking the arrow off its path. It tumbled overhead, and as soon as it landed in the sea behind them, it exploded into an innumerable cluster of Rust-Eater stalks.

Just who is *she?!* thought Bisco, glancing back at the result. *No, I know who she is! I just can't explain it!*

"I think I know who you are," said the woman, mirroring Bisco's own thoughts. Using the jellyshroom stalks growing from the soles of her boots, she stood tall and proud atop the water's surface, glaring back at him. "But I just gotta be sure. Don't want you to die as a result of mistaken identity and resent me in the afterlife. So tell me your name, Mushroom Keeper!"

"You tellin' me you don't know? There ain't a soul in this solar system don't know who I am!"

Even the sharp canine teeth of their respective grins were the exact same. The woman gently placed Sugar down, said "Go hide somewhere, sweetie," and let her go. Sugar looked back and forth between the woman and her father, fearful of what was about to happen.

"In that case, I'll shout it loud and proud, so they can hear me all the way out on whatever backwater planet you're from! I'm one of Earth's two protectors! The world's strongest Mushroom Keeper, Bisco Akaboshi!"

Bisco...Akaboshi!

Something clicked into place as the woman heard that name. She gave a derisive chuckle at the nonsense that Bisco had prefaced it with.

"The world's strongest Mushroom Keeper?"

"Somethin' funny about that, asshole?!"

"No, just a bit strange. You see..."

The woman's smile widened into a canine-baring grin!

"You can't be the strongest," she said, "'cause *I'm* the strongest!!"

Brimming with power, the woman leaped into the air, streaking toward Bisco like a shooting star. Bisco, meanwhile, jumped off Actagawa's forehead, drew his dagger, and slashed at her. Blade and brawny arm crossed above the glittering ocean, and...!

Clanggg!

Whoa?! Sh-she's ridiculously strong!

"Huh? What do you call that?"

Only a handful of Japan's inhabitants could beat Bisco in a contest of raw strength, and one of them was the man's own wife. Therefore, as ridiculous as it sounded, the strange woman was even mightier than she looked. It was only by the skin of his teeth that Bisco dodged the barrage of blows from her meteoric fists, before seizing the opportunity to slice at her tendons with his dagger. But the moment the lizard-claw blade touched her tattoos, not only did it fail to leave a cut—the dagger was bent backward instead.

"What the hell?!"

"You ain't tellin' me that's your best shot, are ya?" the woman jeered. "If you're really my double, then act like it, *Bisco*!!"

The woman countered with a left hook that landed on Bisco's nose, breaking bone and splattering blood. Faced with the force behind that single punch, Bisco finally understood.

There's no doubt. This woman is...!

"Damn right. I'm Bisco Akaboshi, same as you are!"

This new Bisco grabbed our Bisco by the scruff of the neck and pulled his head close.

"I'm here to save my world. And for that, I need your soul!!"

"Glbl!!"

Bisco was plunged into the ocean depths, still held from the back of his head. He raged amid the beautiful marine-blue sea, bubbles spluttering from his mouth.

Rrraaghhh! I can't die...to myself!!

Pulling a syringe from his vial pouch, Bisco stabbed the point into his cloak. The fluorineshrooms within sprouted all across his own body, as well as across that of the woman, with a *pop, pop, pop*, their hydrophobic coating launching the pair out of the ocean back into the sky.

"Phah!"

"You...you don't go down easy!"

"Papa!!"

Driving Actagawa on, Sugar caught her father on the giant crab's back. Bisco looked like a drowned rat, his hair flat and sodden over his eyes, but by rapidly shaking his head like a dog, it returned to normal in an instant.

"Are you okay, Papa?"

"Cough! Hack! Those muscles ain't just for show! She's a monster!"

"Something's strange!" said Sugar, attempting to put her odd feeling into words. "She doesn't feel like a stranger! She feels like a mama! … Even though she's nothing like *my* mama…"

"You might not be entirely wrong about that!" said Bisco, turning once more to face the woman, who stood with arms crossed atop the water's surface. She hadn't taken any *physical* damage, but the sight of Sugar choosing Bisco over her seemed to be causing significant mental distress.

"She's Bisco Akaboshi, a reflection of me from another world!!"

"Whaat?!"

Sugar wasn't sure what to believe at first, but after the strange woman offered no objection to her father's wild claim, her childlike eyes darted back and forth between the two Biscos.

"That's…Papa? I mean…Mama? But wait…Milo's my mama!"

"I ain't surprised you're confused. She looks mostly the same as me, but just look at her eyes! She's nothin' but a mad dog with no respect for society!"

That's why *she looks so much like you!*

All of a sudden, the woman called out to the pair, seemingly fed up.

"Hey! Enough of this. Having two Biscos is too confusing! Back home, me and Milo are known as Red and Blue, the Twinshrooms! Call me that if you've gotta!"

"You want me to call you Red, like the Red Planet?! Ain't you over-sellin' yourself a little?"

"Meanwhile, you can be 'Little Mushroom Boy'! Suits you perfectly," said Red, giving Bisco an appraising look. "Tch. Not a scrap of meat on you. How can you draw a bow like that?"

"I ain't little; you're just big! Don't act like hot shit when you're the trespasser here! Plus, don't forget, we got three guys on our side, while you're all alone!"

"I'm all...alone?"

Red took a large breath, and her tattoos glowed like fire.

"You'll regret saying that," she warned. "'Cause I'm not alone. The hopes and dreams of everyone who died are in my blood!!"

"Wh-what?!"

"Her tattoos aren't just decoration!" Sugar yelled, as fierce storm winds rustled her hair. "They're all people's souls! It's so powerful... but so sad!!"

"Come to me!!"

The power surging within her caused the water to burst outward, like a tidal wave, in all directions. Red summoned up the souls lurking in her tattoos, and they gathered in her hand, forming the shape of a bow.

"Heavencrab Bow!!"

The bow was a manifestation of the great crab Actagawa in all her divine glory, formed of her soul and claw. But it wasn't just her. All those who gave their lives in defense of the dark world returned in spirit, funneling their boundless energy into Red's weapon and her very body.

"Actagawa... I remember now."

Seeing that bow in her hand, Red recalled part of her faded memories—the sight of the great crab's death. But her sentiment lasted only two seconds before she looked up, a fire in her eyes, and glared at Bisco.

"She's getting her powers from those damn tattoos!" Bisco yelled.

"You should be honored," replied Red. "You'll join them soon enough."

"That ain't funny... Whoa, Actagawa!!"

At the sight of Red's weapon, Actagawa suddenly got ornery. It seemed he instinctively recognized its true nature as a reflection of himself and was eager to prove himself the superior of the two, as if butting heads were the only option available.

"Calm down! We gotta work together, or else...!"

Pop, pop.

"Whoa, stop shaking!"

"Papa! Actagawa! Be QUIIIET!"

Sugar bonked each of them on the brow, and the two rowdy boys clammed up in an instant, hanging their heads in shame before the young child.

"Don't get all excited just because you have to fight yourselves! You're like a pair of kids!"

"Sorry."

Pop.

"Now, who's stronger: you or them?"

"Us."

Pop.

"Then have some faith. We'll all do it together, okay? On three! One, two..."

"""*Ultrafaith Bow!!*"""

All three—Bisco, Sugar, and Actagawa—focused in prayer, and their power became spores that coalesced in Bisco's hand, forming a rainbow-colored bow!

"No! That's...!"

Red was disturbed by the weapon's appearance. For the Ultrafaith power—the power to build any future—was one she could no longer call upon in her own world.

"It's the *Ultrafaith Bow*...the power of dreams!"

The *Heavencrab Bow* and the *Ultrafaith Bow*. The two greatest powers of their respective worlds stood opposed across the sea.

"Fine by me!" Red snarled. "Fire away! I'll show you the might of the real world!"

"Whatever you say, asshole!!"

Ka-chew!!

Ker-room!!

The two projectiles collided midair, causing a massive explosion! *Gaboom! Gaboom! Gaboom!* Mushrooms burst to life, parting the sea like Moses and creating platforms in the ocean.

"Wrghhh…"

The blast ruffled Bisco's hair, and he scowled atop Actagawa's back.

"We're…evenly matched?!"

Red couldn't conceal her surprise. Both their most powerful attacks had completely canceled each other out. It all came down to who was faster on the follow-up. And that was…

"Now, Papa!"

"You got it!!"

It was Bisco! Sugar tossed him the Mushy Magic Pole, and with the staff techniques he learned off Pawoo, Bisco went in for a diagonal sweep at Red.

"Take this!"

"Tch!"

Red blocked the strike on her bow, causing a flash of spores that lit up the surroundings. Bisco followed up again and again, with lightning speed, denying Red a chance to fight back.

"I know your weakness now," said Bisco. "Your attacks are as strong as all hell, but in return, you can't make many of 'em!"

This bastard…!!

"Those ghosts hauntin' your tattoos are nothin' but a burden. How'd you expect to keep up with me with them weighin' you down?!"

"A burden…?!"

Faced with Bisco's jade-green eyes just millimeters from her own, Red snarled. One of the tattoos on her right arm began to glow, and sunlight vines burst forth from it, pushing Bisco back!

"Ivy? But that's…!"

"You dare call my tattoos a burden?!"

There was a *Clang!* and Bisco was thrown back. Red surged forward and leaped into the air, carrying none other than the blade of Shishi, the Benibishi king—the Lion's Crimson Sword!

"These are the souls of my friends!!"

Slash!!

"Guhh!"

The peerlessly keen blade of Shishi's sword sliced Sugar's pole in two. Bisco immediately stepped back out of range, but the weapon had already left a shallow gash in his chest.

"Papa!!"

From atop Actagawa's back, Sugar summoned a spore whip, hauling Bisco back into the saddle. Bisco wiped the sweat from his brow and stared at Red in fear and awe.

"Talk about raisin' hell! Just how badly does she want me dead?!"

"Papa…"

"Hmm?"

Sugar's eyes were filled with sadness and pity. Finding it strange that Red had not attacked them yet, Bisco followed the line of her gaze…

"Grh… It burns…"

"Whaa—?!"

Red was squirming in pain, even though Bisco had still failed to land a single hit. So much steam rose off her body, it was as if her very flesh was melting. The vengeful tattoos, meant to be her strength, now caused her to suffer.

Do not fail, Bisco.

Do not fail us…

"Graaaaaaghhh!!"

"She's gone too far! Those tattoos are burning the shit out of her!"

"I…I have to win… It's the only way…"

"Cut it out!" Bisco yelled at her. "We can have a rematch later! You don't have to drive yourself to death!!"

"I have to beat you… I have to *eat* you…!!"

There was no light of reason in her eyes, just a sad flame desperate to accomplish its duty before it fizzled out forever.

"I have to be strong. Strong enough to destroy Rust! Or else…or else it was all for nothing!!"

"Papa!"

Sugar spun around and looked into Bisco's eyes, pleading with him.

"Please. You have to save her!"

"...All right. I will!!"

Bisco nodded. No one understood another Bisco more than Bisco himself. If Red wouldn't listen to words, there was no other option except to knock her out.

"It's your time to shine, Actagawa!"

"Groaaaahhh!!"

Driven only by duty, Red brought back the *Heavencrab Bow* while the flames roasted her body.

"If I can't win, then what was it all for?!"

As Actagawa thundered toward her, she fixed her aim on Bisco, who was seated in the saddle, clutching the reins. Pulling back the arrow as far as she could, she let out a throat-wrenching, heartrending scream!

"They're all DEEEEEAD!!"

"...Red!!"

"Mare! Help us out! *Life Ocean Streeeam!*"

It was fortunate that the battle was taking place over the ocean. Mare's power swirled around Actagawa, granting him the sea god's protection. Then a large whirlpool began to form, with Actagawa at the center. The giant crab raised his big claw, and a waterspout formed around it!

"That power! Give it to meee!!"

Red unleashed the *Heavencrab Bow* once more, but...!

"Come on, Actagawa!"

""*Life Ocean Blizzard!!*""

Red's arrow was sucked into the whirlpools surrounding Actagawa's claw! The Life Ocean Blizzard then engulfed Red, freezing her in a pillar of ice.

"W-waaah?!"

The ice supercooled Red's boiling skin, halting her meltdown, but the mad look in her eyes said she was still out for blood. As she struggled to break free, Actagawa leaped into the air and began spinning like a top.

"Let this cool you off!" Bisco yelled.

"*Crab Technique!*"

"""Suncrab Spin!!"""

Ker-rashhh!

The ice column shattered! Actagawa's spin attack hit with just enough force to knock Red out—a marvelous feat of control. As she flew through the air, ice shards clouding her vision, Red finally parted with the rage that drove her.

Oh...

I guess...I really can't do it alone...

I need you...

Milo...

A single teardrop fell from her jade-green eye and rolled down the tattoo on her face. It was only in the last fleeting moments of consciousness that Red felt herself land in Bisco's arms.

5

Red, sticky death ran down her fingers. It did not slow but only came faster, in great bursts that bloodied Red's clothes.

In her hands, the one she loved grew cold. As Red felt her life slipping away, the despair closed in around her.

"Ahh…!"

"No, no, no…!"

"We have to die together."

"Kill me, you bastard…"

"KILL MEEEE!!"

* * *

"Urgh!"

"Red!"

As the patient twisted and turned on his bed, Milo came running over and examined her closely.

"No! Don't leave me, Milo!!"

She hadn't yet woken up, but her face was contorted in pain, and she ground her teeth mercilessly, clearly having a bad dream.

Red…

Milo didn't know what was causing her so much grief, but for some reason he, too, felt sorrow in the pit of his heart and ran his gentle fingers up Red's neck and across her cheek.

If these tattoos are the souls of people she's lost...

Each time he touched one of Red's tattoos, a slow yet steady heat ran up his finger and through his hand.

How much pain has she been forced to endure?

At Milo's touch, Red's breathing seemed to steady. The boy doctor stared at his patient's face with his starlight eyes, then drew his examination to a close.

"A girl Bisco fell out of a parallel world."

Such was the unsatisfactory explanation Tirol had given to Milo when suddenly showing up at Banryouji Temple with the unconscious Red in tow. Milo was informed of her otherworldly strength, and so he had opted to bolt Red to the bed with stout metal fittings, in case she should try to throw her weight around again. He had even thought to leave the two babies, Sugar and Salt, with their grandma Marie, so they would be safe if anything happened.

I can't speak for her mind... but physically, her recovery is superhuman. There's not a trace of where Actagawa hit her.

"Can we come in yet, Milo?" came a lazy voice from the other room.

"Oh, Tirol!" replied Milo. "Not yet, I still need to do up her clothes..."

"He says it's fine."

"Hmm. Let's see this woman, then..."

"I still don't believe it. How can she be me? She's a monster!"

"Hey, I said not yet! Out, all of you, out!!"

Despite Milo's warning, the three barbarians strode into the room one after the other. They planted themselves before, to the left, and to the right of the sleeping Red, staring down at her like judgmental gods.

The suffocating air clearly pierced the veil of sleep, for Red fidgeted uncomfortably beneath their gazes, and her brow ran slick with sweat.

"Ho-ho, so this is what Akaboshi'd be like as a girl," said Tirol with an appraising glance.

Pawoo, meanwhile, could barely take her eyes off the woman. "I...I don't believe it...!!" she murmured.

"Hey! You two girls! Leave the patient alone."

But as Milo went running over to stop them, Bisco stepped up to examine his alternate-reality self.

"It just ain't me, it just ain't," he muttered. "I mean, look! She's like a wild dog; what part of that looks like me?! You tellin' me that's the face of a law-abidin' citizen?"

"Have you ever looked in the mirror?" asked Tirol.

"You're one to talk about law and order," added Pawoo.

"Are you two serious?! Tell 'em, Milo! I mean, for starters..."

"...she's a woman, yes. I know how you feel, Bisco..."

Milo tried to pull the two girls away, but the pair were so keenly interested in the female Bisco that he couldn't get them to budge.

"...but even from a medical point of view, she's you to a T," he went on. "I think Tirol's hypothesis is correct, and everyone's sex in the dark world is the opposite of what it is here."

"Hrmm..."

"Well, Akaboshi's always been a damsel in distress, though," quipped Tirol.

"And what's that supposed to mean?!" roared Bisco. "Explain it to me right now!"

"You're the one who needs to explain!"

This last voice was of such magnitude that it caused all present to freeze in fear. It was Pawoo, who until that point had been regarding the sleeping Red wordlessly. All of a sudden, she grabbed Bisco by the lapels.

"Look at the female you, Husband! I demand to know why hers are bigger than mine?!"

"What?!"

"Yes, Bisco!" added Milo, joining in. "What's the meaning of this?!"

"How the hell am I supposed to know?!?!"

Urgh...

These riotous voices roused Red from her slumber...and produced an entirely reasonable reaction.

Shut...up...

Her eyes cracked open, but with her mind still hazy, she couldn't recognize anything yet. All she could tell was that she was lying on some kind of bed, with all sorts of equipment attached to her body.

Where am I? What's going on...?

Though Red couldn't discern her circumstance, she instinctively sensed danger. She tried to move, only to find she was pinned in place by the wrists, neck, and torso.

This...

This is bad.

They're gonna kill me!!

"Rooooaaaaaaaghhh!!"

Snapp!

Red's tattoos shone bright crimson, and the bickering friends all spun around to face her, ready for anything. Red, meanwhile, summoned all of her strength and lifted her bed over her head.

"Daaaaaghhh!!"

With a primal scream, she threw the furniture. The others jumped aside, letting the bed lodge itself in the wall.

"Eep! She's awake!"

"Dammit!"

"Bisco! Stay! Please calm down, ma'am!"

Milo stepped between the two sides, eager to de-escalate this confrontation before either of the Biscos did anything rash.

"We're not your enemy, Red. We're on your side! You've been through a lot, we know that. But I can help you! You just have to trust me!"

"Wh-who...are you...?"

"I'm Milo Nekoyanagi!"

Milo Nekoyanagi.

Cheerful and smart. Bright and sunny. Red could never mistake the voice of her dear partner, even if it was a little deeper than usual.

"I'm Bisco's partner!" said Milo. "And I went to school! So there's nothing to worry about!"

"Milo…? That…that's not…possible…"

Red looked into his eyes, those kindly, panda-marked eyes that had watched over the recovery of so many a patient, and a nightmare scratched the back of her mind.

That voice. That warmth. It couldn't be him.

"Because…Milo… She… She…di…"

"Watch out!" cried Bisco. "She's losin' it!"

"Ma'am, please try to calm down!"

"Don't speak to me…in her voice!!"

Forbidden memories melted the walls of her soul, and Red's tattoos emitted waves of heat that launched everybody else back.

"Aaagh!! My research notes!" Tirol's braids stood on end as she watched Banryouji's store of knowledge go up in flames. "Milo, yer voice ain't calming her; it's makin' her even angrier!"

"B-but why?!"

"Musta been 'cause she saw through your lies," said Bisco. "She really is just as perceptive as me."

"What lies?! What's that supposed to mean?!"

"Get back, boys!" Pawoo announced her presence with one swing of her staff and stepped forward to keep the peace. "Remaining awake is only causing Ms. Red more pain. We need to knock her out again! As Bisco's spouse, I, Pawoo Nekoyanagi, will take on this responsibility!"

"Pawoo…?!"

Upon hearing that name, Red gasped and looked up, but her eyes had not fully healed, and she could not see clearly.

"Apologies!" yelled Pawoo, brandishing her staff. "Please forgive me! Hi-yah!!"

Pawoo leaped into the air, preparing to unleash her powerful Whitesnake Arts. Red was in a daze, unable to block, and Pawoo's strike connected with her neck!

However…

Clanggg!!

"…What?!"

"Grrr…!!"

Pawoo's aim had been true, but even the most vulnerable of Red's muscles were like tempered steel, causing the staff to become bent out of shape.

Even without her sight, it would be simple for Red to return a killing blow at this distance. Pawoo had poured her all into that one strike, and now she realized her mistake.

I…I've failed!

She gritted her teeth, preparing for the inevitable counterblow, when…!

"Pawoo!!"

Red lunged at her, not with her fists but with her arms! She wrapped them around her, drawing the bewildered woman into a soft and warm embrace.

"I missed you so much…!" she said, nuzzling her cheek.

"…You did?"

""""Whaaat?!""""

Every soul in the room was utterly flabbergasted.

"I thought you died… I thought you…hmm? …Did you put on weight? You feel all…womanly!"

Red attempted to examine the surprised Pawoo, then stepped between her and everyone else in the room.

"Watch out, Pawoo!" she said. "There's something wrong with this world! It might be another one of Rust's illusions!"

"Hold on, Ms. Red! You've got it all wrong! I'm not…"

"Hmm? Why are you talking weirdly? I'm your wife, for crying out loud. Call me Bisco, like you always do!"

Pawoo had no idea what to do. In her confusion, Red had turned her back. From this position, Pawoo could knock her out with one clean chop to the back of the neck.

"That's it!" cried Milo. "She's wide open! Get her, Pawoo!"

"What are you standin' around for?! Do it already!"

However…

"Don't worry, Pawoo. I'll keep you safe, whatever happens!"

Hearing those words, in something like her husband's voice, touched Pawoo's heart in a place her brain couldn't reach.

"…Yes…my love…"

""What are you doing?!?!""

Her cheeks flushed, and she swooned into Red's embrace. Bisco and Tirol yelled at her in chorus. It was only Milo, with a wry smile plastered on his face, who somehow understood how his sister felt.

"What's yer wife playin' at, Akaboshi?! She's missin' her chance!!"

"Sh…she's fallen for Red's wiles!" said Bisco, sweating beads. "Hey! Red! First you come into our universe uninvited, then you steal my wife?! Who the hell do you think you are?!"

"Well said," said Milo, grinning at Bisco. "Are you just going to let her get away with that? And we're in Banryouji Temple, don't forget. It's basically sacrilege! Give her what for, Bisco!"

As if pulled by his partner's invisible strings, Bisco flew into a rage against Red.

"You dare make a pass at Pawoo right in front of me?! You should be ashamed!!"

"What's so strange about that?! Pawoo's my husband!"

"Are you blind?! That's my wife!!"

?!?!?!

Pawoo took in the strange scene unfolding before her.

Two Biscos, fighting over me?!?!

Her already lovestruck heart could take it no longer, and…

"Whuh…"

Her soul slipped from her body, and Pawoo hit the floor, unconscious. Both Biscos crowded around her, concerned.

""Pawoo!""

Good for her, thought Milo, a half smile on his lips, when Tirol suddenly slapped him around the back of the head.

"There's nothin' good about it!" she yelled, quickly realizing she was the only sensible person in the room.

What do we do?! she thought, biting her fingernails. *At this rate, Akaboshi and Red are gonna have it out again, and they'll ruin the whole temple!*

But just as she puzzled over it, Tirol heard a voice.

Tirol.

Tirol, can you hear me?

"Huh???"

Tirol looked around, but nobody in the room seemed like the voice's owner.

"Did you say something, Milo?"

"No?"

"Huh? Must be losin' it…"

Take my memories, Tirol.

"There it is again! You messin' with me, Panda Boy?!"

"Calm down! I don't know what you're talking about!"

"This ain't the time for pranks! We need to stop that other Akaboshi before…"

Listen to me.

A terrible shock has sealed off Red's memories.

If you share mine with her, she should turn back to normal.

Take my power, and do what I cannot, Tirol!

"Th-this ain't Milo! Whose voice is this?!"

"What's wrong, Tirol?!"

"Someone's in my head! Aaaaghhh!"

The next moment, Tirol felt unknown knowledge filling the cracks in her mind, and her intellect swelled to two, four, ten times its original size. A pink aura engulfed her, causing her jellyfish braids to float. The two Biscos stopped what they were doing and stared at her in shock.

"What the—?!"

"Tirol?!"

"M-my memories! That's right! These are *my* memories!!"

The quick-witted Tirol understood in a flash that the *other* Tirol was entrusting the contents of his mind to her. Raising the light of remembrance over her head, she unleashed the memories contained within.

"Everyone, see this! **Launch:Memory:Recollect!!**"

A wave of energy spread out from her, enclosing the entire temple in a hemispherical dome! Bisco and Milo saw everything go white and felt themselves approaching a new scene, just beyond the veil of consciousness.

* * *

"Kill...me."

"Is that your wish, Twinshroom Red? Very well. In my boundless grace, I shall grant it."

The cogwheels around the Rust god's arm began to spin. Soon, his attack would vaporize Red without a trace, but she couldn't bring herself to care, much less stand. All she could do was stare down her impending death.

"Farewell," said Rust, but just as he was about to fire...

"Laaaunch! City:Maker:Megalopolis!!"

Kaboom!!

Conjured by the hidden arts of Banryouji Temple, an office block building sprouted from the ground, striking Rust's arm with such force that it tore it clean off. The dismembered limb sailed through the air and landed in the distant forests of Mt. Fuji, where it exploded in a ball of flame.

"Hmm."

"Hands off Akaboshi, rust bucket!"

It was Tirol! He ran up to Red and pulled her away from the body at her feet and away from Rust.

"Get ahold of yourself, Akaboshi! Where's Milo?! What happened to her?!"

Tirol shook Red by the shoulders, but when he noticed the blood dripping down her front, he could guess the rest. He bit his lip, hoping he could wish away the cruel fate that had befallen his good friend, but then he steeled himself for what was at stake.

"You can't give up now, Akaboshi!" he yelled. "Akaboshi! Listen to me!"

"..."

"Akaboshi! Listen to me! Can you hear me?!"

Red's eyes were hollow, and it wasn't clear whether she even realized that Tirol was there. As Tirol frantically tried to shake her out of it, N'nabadu looked on in glee.

"Who's that small one?" he asked, apparently without a hint of irony. *"One of Banryouji's rats? A friend of the Mushroom Keepers, I presume. Do away with them, will you, Lord Rust? I can hardly imagine a more depressing sight."*

"I can. You."

"S-s-surely you jest, my lord!"

"Stand, Akaboshi! Remember, you still have a son to protect!!"

Tirol shook Red by the shoulders, but it was clear she wasn't listening.

It's no good. The shock is too great to handle. I must partition off her memories for a while!

Tirol muttered a spell underneath his breath and placed his glowing hand to Red's forehead.

"Launch:Memory:Isolate!"

Using his mind-altering techniques, Tirol sealed off Red's unhappy memories where they could do no harm. Rust watched this all play out with an expression of minimal concern, before re-forming his missing limb.

"That should do it!"

Then Tirol heard a jubilant voice from behind.

"Do not meddle. That woman has been crushed. She has offered her soul to me. Once a proud, noble being, she now begs for death. What could be crueler than granting it to her?"

"Shut up!!"

"Out of my way, little jellyfish."

"Boot! City:Maker:Train!!"

Tirol spun around and unleashed his mantra, and a Yamanote Line train car shot from the bare rock and hurtled into Rust.

"Oh?"

"Wh-what's this?! Gwaaagh!!"

Ker-room!

Rust didn't even try to dodge the train. It hit him straight in the stomach, catapulting him far into the distant hillside in a plume of dust and smoke.

Tirol coughed up a mixture of blood and screws.

"*Cough! Cough!* Dammit…!!"

"…Ti…rol…?"

Upon witnessing his suffering, Red had the light return to her jade-green eyes, and her tattoos began to glow once more.

"Tirol! What's wrong with you?!"

"So you finally noticed, Akaboshi…!"

Red tried to help Tirol up, but more than half of the boy's skin had been replaced with an unfeeling cityscape. Telegraph poles grew out of him, sparking. It looked incredibly painful, but Tirol only wore a satisfied smile.

"D-did we fail?" Red asked. "Dammit, my memory's gone!"

"We haven't failed," Tirol replied. "You're still alive. And I'll use my final technique to get you to safety."

"Safety?! What are you talking about?! If we don't end this here

and now, we're all doomed! Nobody in the world can face up to Rust!!"

"Correction: Nobody in *this* world," said Tirol. "Those at Banryouji anticipated this scenario and left me with one final trick up my sleeve: Akasha Tripper, a technique capable of sending people to parallel worlds."

"Wh-what do you mean, parallel worlds?"

"Listen carefully, Akaboshi. I'm going to send you to the light world, which exists in parallel with our dark one. There you'll meet another Red—another Bisco Akaboshi. You must use your absorption technique to devour the other Akaboshi's soul, thereby gaining enough power to defeat the Rust god!"

It was all so sudden. Bisco had never heard this theory of parallel worlds before, and even if her memory hadn't been hazy, she would have been hard-pressed to understand and digest it. But she understood one thing: her mission. The task Tirol had given her. It burned in her heart, never to be forgotten.

I have to find the other me...and devour them!

"We must hurry, Akaboshi! Rust is on his way."

Tirol looked to the distance, where Rust battled the serpentine form of the Yamanote Line train. Watching the wicked god tear into the metal with his bare hands, he realized time was running out. And so, while rapidly succumbing to citification, Tirol began intoning his ultimate technique.

"Akasha:Tripper:Setup. Calculating... Calculating... Constructing... Searching... Reconstructing..."

"Tirol! No! You can't take it!" cried Red, as Tirol's body cracked apart under the pressure of the spell. "Stop it! You don't have to get yourself killed just for me!!"

"That's my choice to make. Do you have a problem with that?"

"But...you've always hated me!"

"I don't bother arguing with people I hate."

Tirol reached for Red's face and, with a thumb, wiped away her flowing tears. He took in for the last time the features of the

woman with whom he had often quarreled, and he left her with a proud smile.

"You know," he said, "this is the first time I've ever seen you cry."

"..."

"It doesn't suit you."

With his spell completed, Tirol placed his hand on Red's cheek. As soon as he touched her, the woman was engulfed in a pale-green light.

"This is farewell, Akaboshi. Go easy on the other me, if you can handle that!"

"Don't do this, Tirol! Don't leave me alone!!"

"Just go! *Akasha Tripper!!*"

Clad in the green light of the spell, Red shot into the air like a rocket, then streaked across the sky like a meteor.

"What in the world is that?!" asked the bewildered N'nabadu. *"That light... Is that Akasha Tripper?! Did the humans finally perfect a means to travel between dimensions?!"*

"Should I shoot it down?" asked Rust.

"Please do!"

Rust nodded and fired off a supersonic cogwheel that followed after Red. The greenish streak, however, opened up a hole in space-time and disappeared inside, so that by the time the cogwheel caught up, Red had disappeared from this reality entirely.

"Curses! Red has eluded us!" cried N'nabadu, clutching his head and stamping his feet in midair. *"Of course! Her aim must be to gather souls in the other dimension! I should have known they'd have another trick up their sleeves!"*

"So what you're saying is, you failed to predict this, fly?"

"Oh, forgive me, my lord!!"

"Ah-ha-ha-ha! Idiots!" chortled Tirol, bent over with painful laughter. "You underestimated me just because I'm little, didn't you? Well, now you know! A jellyfish's poison is slow but effective!!"

"Heh. How amusing."

Rust seemed to take Tirol's pointed words in stride, but N'nabadu went entirely crimson with rage.

"Y-you think you've outwitted me, you tricky little child?! I'll get you for this! Your death will be most painful! Lord Rust! Finish him off!"

"Very well."

This is as far as I go, huh…?

His task was complete.

"Farewell, little jellyfish."

"Die, die, diiie!!"

He was not afraid. Tirol had given his life for that of his friend and regretted nothing. Staring down his impending death, he channeled all his remaining life force into one last technique!

"O fallen of Banryouji. Grant me peerless wisdom in my final moments! *Launch:City:Makeeer!!*"

* * *

"""…Haah!!"""

Bisco and Milo came to their senses and turned to each other.

"Wh-what was that?" asked Milo.

"They were someone's final memories," said Bisco. "But whose?"

"Mine."

The two turned to look at Tirol, who sounded oddly subdued. She wiped her tears with the edge of her sleeve before silently placing a hand to her breast.

"I gave my own life to send Red here," she went on. "What an idiot. What's the point of saving the world if I'm dead…?"

"What do you mean, you gave your life?!"

"Your pulse seems normal to me, Tirol!!"

"Keep up, you numbskulls! I ain't talkin' about *this* me!"

Tirol launched herself at the dim-witted pair, while Red muttered to herself in the background.

"…I remember now," she said. "Tirol sacrificed herself to keep me safe."

After seeing what had happened from Tirol's point of view, Red began to make sense of her own jumbled memories. They hadn't all returned yet, but the jade-green light was back in her eyes.

"That means this is the light world," she reasoned. "All the people who died in my world are still alive here…"

"Red!"

"I'm sorry. I thought this was an illusion created by the Rust god."

Though she appeared to be capable of rational thought once more, there was a touch more sadness in Red's voice now. She looked around and, seeing Pawoo, dashed over to help her to her feet.

"I'm sorry, Pawoo," she whispered. "Did I frighten you?"

"M-Ms. Red…"

"I thought we were reunited again… I just got a little excited."

Red flashed a smile, but her eyes said how she really felt.

"Go on," she said. "Return to your husband."

Pawoo couldn't take the loneliness in Red's words. Before she knew it, she was hugging the woman tightly. She felt Red tremble in shock. For several seconds, neither of them moved a muscle. Pawoo listened to Red's heartbeat, then opened her own eyes, which were quivering as well.

6

"I've finally located the coordinates of the light world!"

N'nabadu tapped away at the keys on his personal device. By analyzing the traces left by Tirol's Akasha Tripper, Rust's insect servant had succeeded in pinning down Red's location in four-dimensional hyperspace.

"Let me just project an image... My, what a beautiful world! Just look at this, my lord! This is the world that lies parallel to our—erk!"

"Silence, fly."

Rust brushed away the buzzing nuisance with a flick of his wrist, before soothing the child who had woken up and begun crying in his arms.

That child was, of course, Sugar Akaboshi. N'nabadu had found and extracted the baby boy, hoping to use him as a bargaining chip against Red. To that end, the child remained unharmed.

"You've woken the baby," said Rust, unamused. "Are you incapable of staying silent?"

"Waah... Waahh...!"

Sugar's voice issued from the roof of a city building and echoed across the peak of Mt. Fuji. The building was the one left by Tirol's final attack, and Rust swung his legs from its edge as he tried to calm the child down.

"There, there, don't cry..."

"Come, my lord. That is the child of your sworn enemy!" N'nabadu shot Sugar a nasty glare, as though jealous of the affection the baby was receiving. *"He is useful to us, yes, but we needn't bother ourselves with his care!"*

"It is a weak creature. Such care is only proper."

Rust watched as the upset child slowly calmed down, but he did so without a single change to his own emotionless expression. N'nabadu, meanwhile, silently seethed as the child monopolized his master's affections in return for doing absolutely nothing.

"...It has gone back to sleep," said Rust at last, letting out a sigh. "So what was it you wanted?"

"My lord, as I was saying, I have reverse engineered the boy's space-time magic. Look at this footage."

Rust looked as indicated and came face-to-face with an unknown vista.

"What is this world...?"

"That is the light world, my lord. It is a reflection of our own world, but it has not yet succumbed to ruin."

"..."

The vision showed a bright and glittering land, bathed in sunlight. Between the ruined buildings and rusted tanks grew lush and strong vegetation, while animals warred over scarce resources in an eternal song of life and death.

...It's beautiful.

Rust let out a sigh, captivated by the sight. Then he shifted his gaze to the sea of rust statues stretched out before him. Nothing but a breeding ground for dead dreams. There was nothing of interest left in this soul-drained world.

"Why is such a beautiful world as yet untouched?"

"Well, my lord..." N'nabadu stared at the screen of his device. *"It appears that, for whatever reason, there is no Rust god in this world. Perhaps he—or she—was defeated, or perhaps they were never created in the first place."*

"Which means I can have all those delicious souls to myself,"

said Rust, the excitement in his voice growing by the second. "Those proud, strong-willed warriors, all mine!"

"Oh, you are most malevolent, my lord! ... Wait, do you mean to tell me you intend to travel there?"

"Of course. Make it so, fly. Now."

"Be reasonable, my lord! I've only just managed to create a stable connection!"

However, despite his protests, N'nabadu set about at once making good on his master's wishes, pressing buttons on his device like mad.

"Understand this, my lord. Without you there to cull their numbers, we shall expect to find Mushroom Keepers aplenty in this new world. You may be mighty, but you cannot expect to take on the whole tribe by yourself!"

"Figure something out, then."

"The biggest threat of all comes in the form of that world's Sugar."

N'nabadu cast a rotten glare at the baby asleep in Rust's arms.

"It appears that in that world, the child is a mushroom god, a counterpart of sorts to yourself. Of course, it scarcely bears mentioning whose might is greater, but direct combat is still unadvised! We don't know what could happen!"

"Figure something out, then."

"Goodness me!"

Despite his overblown reaction, the words of his master were more or less what N'nabadu had expected to hear. He approached Rust's ear as quietly as he could and meekly gave his proposal.

"In that case, my lord, may I suggest you do not invade immediately but instead send me to scout ahead? Using Akasha Tripper, I can thin the Mushroom Keeepers in advance of your arrival."

"You have a plan to deal with them?"

"I do, my lord... But I shall need some of your souls... About ten thousand or so ought to do it..."

"I should have known."

Rust gave a look of obvious displeasure. It wasn't so much

parting with the souls itself that was the problem, rather the method of doing so.

"Very well. Get it over with."

"As you wish."

With Rust's permission, N'nabadu happily flew into his master's ear, searching for the souls he required from among the endless maelstrom swirling within.

"Aaah! It feels so good, swimming around in all these souls! Which should I take? This? Oh, this one looks pretty, too!"

"Hurry up, fly, before I grind you into dust!!"

"Please wait, my lord! I have not yet decided on a form."

It probably went without saying that Rust did not appreciate having a small fly buzzing around inside his head, and he was becoming steadily more irritable as a result. But just as the veins started to form on his forehead and it seemed with a little more effort he really could squash N'nabadu through sheer force of will...

"Oh! This soul has an exceedingly strong wish! Body Change!"

...there was a *Plop!* and a figure even larger than Rust himself somehow tumbled out of his ear.

"What a good soul," the figure said. *"What do you think of my new form, my lord?"*

"..."

While his manner of speaking remained unchanged, N'nabadu's voice had become that of a young man—the owner of the soul he had snatched from his master's stores. He had white fluffy hair and peculiar garb, and his left eye was jade-green and made of glass, held open at all times by a bizarre setup of straps.

N'nabadu admired himself in a reflection before saying, *"My, how handsome I look! I really struck the jackpot here!"*

"A pity it doesn't change that you are still a fly."

"Hah-hah-hah!" N'nabadu chortled, then bowed to his master. *"Well then, my lord, I must be off. Rest assured that by the time you set foot in the light world, the Mushroom Keepers shall present no impediment."*

"Good."

"So please, until I call for you..."

"Yes. I shall stay right here."

"And I shall return with good tidings, my lord."

N'nabadu muttered the words of his spell under his breath and scratched at thin air with his elongated nails, opening a rift in space-time, into which he stepped and disappeared.

Rust watched it all go down with minimal interest, then sighed and, still feeling the effects of the fly's presence, struck his ear a couple of times with his palm.

"Waah! Waah!"

"Oh, don't cry, infant. There, there..."

Rust turned to the crying child and plucked a single memory from the sea of souls swirling around in his head.

The dead world was completely silent, save for the god's irredeemably off-key singing. Yet somehow, perhaps through sheer grit alone, the infant Sugar managed to fall asleep.

7

Ding.

"Ochagama..."

Pawoo lit a stick of incense and kneeled before the shrine of Tirol's grandfather (he died a while back from eating too much daifuku).

"The prodigal daughter of Banryouji has become one of the greatest minds in Japan. I have seen how she carries on your great legacy, so please, rest easy in the afterlife..."

"Shut the heck up, Pawoo! I can't concentrate!"

Tirol waved the incense smoke out of her eyes and resumed tapping away madly on her keyboard.

Taktaktaktaktak...!!

"Grr, this spaghetti code's makin' my head spin!!"

With her headband, winter coat, and thick glasses, Tirol looked just like a student cramming for university exams.

"That Rust god's no amateur programmer, that's for sure! I gotta patch the bugs in Akasha Tripper to keep him out, but I can't believe *I* wrote this crud! What was I thinking?! Grrr! Couldn't Grandpappy have stuck around for another six months...?!"

By combining her knowledge with that of her dark world counterpart, Tirol had become a super-genius overnight. However, that still didn't mean she could make sense of a dimension-warping computer program without tremendous effort.

Perhaps Pawoo felt sorry for her to some extent, for she sat about, desperate to make herself useful. "What should I help you with?" she asked. "Just say the word, and I'll do it!"

While Tirol was unable to lift her fingers from the keyboard, Pawoo replaced an ice pack on the girl's forehead. Like a mother looking after her hardworking child, she had even left some tea, snacks, and rock-hard rice balls on Tirol's desk.

"You will get blood clots in your legs if you keep at this much longer," she advised. "Try lying on your side for a bit, and I'll massage your shoulders."

"Leave me alone!! Your last massage nearly snapped me in half!!"

"Aww..."

"Just sit in the corner, where you can't break anything," said Tirol, shooing her away, and Pawoo trudged over there sullenly.

"Are you saying I'm useless?!" she wailed. "My husband said he didn't need any more people, and Marie won't let me look after Salt, either! What am I supposed to do with my burning desire to help?!"

Pawoo, the Whirling Steel, was feared throughout the land for being as strong as she was simple, but right now she was as unthreatening as a little girl, desperate to be needed. This desire was a core part of her, and it had been why she so eagerly joined the Vigilante Corps in the past, but it meant that she couldn't stand being idle while her friends and family suffered.

Tirol raised her specs, scratched her head, and sighed. "Don't worry," she said. "You'll get your turn."

"Really?!"

"Yeah. After this, something's comin' up that only you can handle."

* * *

"All right, both sides, relax. Make sure you're holding on tight. Ready? Don't start yet..."

"Gettin' scared yet, Red? You can use both hands if it'll make you feel better."

"Ha! Keep talking, little mushroom. You ain't shit without your partner's help, and when I'm done with you, you'll realize that."

"Oh, now you've said it, asshole!"

"So what if I did, punk?"

"Ready...go!"

As soon as Milo took his hands away, both Red and Bisco flared with mushroom spores! They had decided to settle their differences with a good old-fashioned arm wrestle.

""Grrrr...!!""

Veins bulged in both arms. While Red was clearly the sturdier built of the two, her strength and Bisco's were about equal, and for a while, neither player surrendered a millimeter. In the end, it was the stone they were contesting atop that yielded first, letting out a magnificent crack, sending each flying inward and over the other's shoulders, with Red landing in the temple pond, while Bisco hit a stone lantern and smashed it into tiny pieces. Milo calmly turned to a blackboard and chalked up the result.

"*Arm Wrestling: Draw*," he wrote. "*Sigh.*"

His entry came at the end of a long list.

FOOT RACING: DRAW.

BREATH HOLDING: DRAW.

WEIGHT LIFTING: DRAW.

KANJI MEMORIZATION: 0 POINTS EACH.

COOK-OFF: UNMENTIONABLE.

CHESS: CANCELED, AS NEITHER PLAYER COULD UNDERSTAND THE RULES.

POETRY SLAM: TOO PECULIAR TO JUDGE.

HORROR MOVIE WATCH-OFF: 0 SECONDS EACH.

Milo was slowly realizing that the two Biscos were identical to an unsettling degree.

"We can't keep doing this; we'll be at it all night." He sighed. "Can't we just agree you're both equal? You're both two halves of the same whole, so who's to say which one's better?"

"I am, and it's me!"

"No, it's me!"

Bisco and Red leaped to their feet and instantly grappled once more, butting their heads together.

"You've done well to keep up with me, little mushroom. Out of respect, I'll let you be my apprentice!"

"Say that when you've won a single match, Red! Next is mushroom raisin'!"

"Just you watch! This whole country'll be a fungal forest when I'm DONE!"

"Come on! Cut it out already!" yelled Milo as the pair geared up for their next fight. The two seemed less like rivals and more like a pair of perfectly matched troublemakers.

"Milo! Help me use the Mantra Bow!" yelled Red. "I'll win this next one for sure!"

"Whaat?! B-but…"

"Hey, hands off my partner, asshole!" Bisco shouted. "Find your own!"

"I'm just borrowing him for a bit; you don't have to be so stingy! Besides, there's only one person in the whole universe who knows how to treat Milo right, and that's me!"

"Up yours! It's me!"

Somebody help!

Milo suddenly found himself feeling like the rope in a tug-of-war. As the two brutish Biscos pulled him this way and that, it dawned on him…

They're going to tear me apart!

But just as he felt his consciousness fade, he was thrown to one side, as the lighter Bisco suddenly and inexplicably let go.

"Ah-ha-ha! Did you give up?" taunted Red. "W-wait, what's wrong?!"

"Bisco!"

Still not understanding what had just happened, Bisco looked from side to side in confusion. Red helped him to his feet, whereupon he realized his whole body was flickering with a golden light.

"Huh? I was holding on, but Milo suddenly slipped away. What happened?!"

"H-hey, don't look now, but I think there's something wrong with your hands!" cried Red.

"What's wrong with you? What's got you so spooked?" said Bisco, looking down. "What the hell?! My hand…it's gone!!"

Bisco was astonished to see that his right wrist suddenly terminated in a cloud of spores. There was no blood or anything of the sort, but that only made the sight even more unsettling.

"Bisco!! What's happened to you?!"

"I…I dunno! My hand just…"

"…Could it be?!"

Red took a closer look at Bisco's wrist, and her face stiffened. She realized that only the villainous N'nabadu could be responsible.

But before she could warn the others…

"Gyaaaaaghh!! Come quick, you three!!"

Who should come running and screaming onto the scene but Tirol, still wearing her bottle-bottom specs. Unable to stop herself in time, she crashed into Bisco, knocking him over and falling under his right arm.

"That was close! Wait, Akaboshi, what happened to your hand?!"

"Tirol!" shouted Red. "N'nabadu's behind this; I'm sure of it! He's cast some kind of curse on us!"

"I think I know the cause," said Tirol. "Feast yer peepers on this!"

Three pairs of eyes converged on the screen in Tirol's hands. Her computer had just finished modeling the structure of the two worlds, closely intertwined in a double helix like a strand of DNA.

"I see a black helix and a white one," said Milo.

"Yeah. The white one is this world, the light world, and the black one is Red's world."

"I see!"

"Now here's the kicker. Take a closer look at the white one."

"'"???"'"

Steam was already pouring from the two Akaboshis' ears as they struggled to keep up. Milo glanced at them, then back at the screen, where he noticed something gray wrapped around the white helix.

"What's that...thing attached to our world?!"

"Looks like a snake, right? That's the Svapna Akasha!!"

Tirol continued tapping away at her keyboard as she explained.

"It's a fake world that N'nabadu created. He's trying to overwrite this world's history with an invented one!"

"I see...," muttered Red. While Bisco remained as glassy-eyed as ever, she was wise to the ways of her old nemesis. "He knows he can't take you on in a fair fight, so he's making a world where he won't need to—one where both of you are already dead!"

"He's trying to write us out of existence?!"

"And that's the Svapna Akasha...!"

The scale of what was being said boggled the two boys' minds, but they understood the gist—if they didn't stop the fly's plan, their very world would be rewritten!

"How are we supposed to stop that?!" asked Bisco. "All we know how to do is shoot things until they stop movin'!"

"Oh, well, we had a good run," offered Milo. "As long as we die together, I don't mind. So how long do we have left?"

"At least try to fight your fate a little!!" Tirol yelled.

Uh-oh, thought Red. *If these guys disappear, so do my chances of beating Rust!*

She turned to Bisco and pushed aside her guilt with grim determination.

Before that happens...I gotta eat him!

"Okay, calm down, y'all!" came Tirol's bold voice. The two boys and Red all turned to face her. "It ain't the end of the world just yet! I'm the new head priestess of Banryouji Temple here, and that means I have a plan!"

"'"Let's hear it!"'"

"The Svapna Akasha is an invented world, which means it needs someone to imagine it into existence. If you guys go in and beat up that guy, then the world will crumble with him!"

"*'Go in'?* you're talkin' like we have a way to travel between worlds!"

"We do! Look!!"

Tirol snapped her fingers, and from beneath an unsuspecting floor mat came a loud rumble, as a strange pedestal rose out of the floor.

"This," she declared, pointing at the item atop it, "is Mr. Brain! It's a device that amplifies mantra power!"

It was some sort of heavy-looking device to be worn around the head. Countless cables fell off the back of it, which were connected to an old Buddhist shrine.

"By wearing this," Tirol explained, "I can access the minds of all my ancestors here at Banryouji! With power like that, even I can learn to control Akasha Tripper!"

"Y-you made this just now?!"

Bisco was used to the girl's quick wits and resourcefulness, but this took the cake. Even an amateur like him could see that the scale of the device was beyond normal reckoning.

"I hate to say it," said Bisco, "but I guess I underestimated you. Well, Red? Our Tirol's not bad, eh?"

"Heh. And here I thought she was just a little troublemaker."

"Well, she is that, too."

"Shut up, hedgehog-hair! You ready, Milo? I can only transport up to three people. And outta you and the Akaboshis, you're the only one I trust. Make sure they find the one dreamin' up the Svapna Akasha!"

"T-Tirol, are you really going to do this?!" asked Milo, the only one capable of communicating with the girl on her level. "You can't! The more powerful the mantra, the greater the effects on the user! If you do this, you could die!"

"Ahhh, why is it only you who ever looks out for me, Panda Boy?"

Tirol slipped coyly into Milo's arms, before flashing him a defiant grin.

"You don't need to worry about me," she said. "You really think I'm gonna go down so easy?"

"No, but…"

"Everythin's ready for ya. Now get goin'. Banryou Tetsujin!"

"Enlightenment achieved."

"Prepare to crush evil."

"Banryou Tetsujin, moving out!!"

The powerful voice of a woman echoed throughout Banryouji, and then the entire temple began to shake. Eventually, the structure cracked open, and out of the ground, through the roof tiles, came an enormous figure!

""Whoa! The temple's falling apart!""

"Get out of there, you two!!"

Everyone ran out of the temple as fast as their legs could carry them, and they turned to look at what had emerged, which was large enough to blot out the sun. When they saw what it was, the two boys' mouths fell agape. It was an enormous Tetsujin robot, which had transformed out of the temple itself!

"Tirol, what is that?!"

"That's the true form of Banryouji Temple! We call it: Banryou Tetsujin!"

Tirol squinted into the bright light given off by the being's halo.

"Banryou Tetsujin possesses a Mantra Engine, capable of converting the faith of its pilot into energy," Tirol explained. "That should be more than enough to power the Akasha Tripper!"

"Pilot? Who'd be crazy enough to—?"

"That would be me!"

""P-Pawoo?!""

The boys' hair stood up in fright. Meanwhile, the robot began making signs with its eight arms, causing its halo to glow successively brighter, until the four people below had to fall prone, eyes squeezed shut.

"For you, my dear brother," came Pawoo's echoing voice once more,

"and for my dear husband as well, I, Pawoo Nekoyanagi, shall do everything I can to help! See how the strength of my devotion fills the Mantra Engine to its brim!"

Pawoo sat cross-legged in the cockpit, fingers linked, while a bright light engulfed her, causing her hair to flutter. The intense concentration caused a greasy sweat to dribble down her shoulders, while her long eyelashes trembled atop her tightly squeezed eyes.

"Rghhh... Just a little more, and we'll have all the energy we need..."

"Y-you idiot! What are you doing, Pawoo?! Get down from there! You'll—!"

But just as Bisco tried to dissuade her, Red caught him by the scruff and yanked him back.

"Thanks, Pawoo! I love you!" she shouted. "And I can feel your love for me, too. With that love at my back, there's no way I'll lose!"

"Yes...my husband..."

"Wh-whaaaat?!"

Bisco wasn't sure what annoyed him more: his swooning wife or Red's burly muscles holding him back. Either way, it made his blood boil.

"Take that back!" he yelled. "There's only one dude bad enough to be Pawoo's wife!!"

"Yeah, and that's me."

"No, it's me! It's me, dammit, me! Because..."

Bisco howled like a kid desperate to keep his parent!

"I love Pawoo more than yooou!!"

Upon Pawoo hearing Bisco's heartfelt admission, her eyes shot open.

"Rrrroooaaaahhh!!"

In a flash, the mantra energy went from 98 percent to 100 percent, then to 200 percent, then to 500 percent and rising rapidly!

"L-look at that! Wife Energy at one thousand eighty percent!!" Pawoo cheered.

"It's *mantra* energy," jabbered Tirol, before leaping onto the Tetsujin's open palm. "I figured it would go like this; that's why I put you in the pilot seat. Glad to see ya didn't let me down."

"Tirol! Activate the Akasha Tripper while I'm still brimming with love!"

"You got it!"

Tirol made a few signs with her hands, and the mantra energy poured out of the halo. Upon contact with the air, there was a loud *Gwomm!* and a large, dark void appeared in the sky above the robot's head.

"All right! The subspace tunnel's open!"

It was like someone had carved a patch of night into the daytime sky. The interior of the subspace tunnel looked like a tube of stars, filled with streaking meteorites.

"Wow… So that tunnel leads to an alternate dimension…," said Milo, the sight tickling his scientific curiosity. "…Wait, we're going already?! We haven't even done anything to prepare!"

"*Whatever the world may be like on the other side…*," said Pawoo, floating in meditation within the cockpit. *"Remember that it is merely a false world! You three are true to life, born of the land and of your mother's wombs! Whatever's waiting for you doesn't stand a chance!"*

"Let's do this, Pawoo!" yelled Tirol. As she signed with her hands, the Banryou Tetsujin followed with its eight arms!

"Blessings upon your journey…"

""Launch:Akasha:Tripper!!""

The two girls screamed in unison, and Bisco and Milo were suddenly engulfed in a warm light, before shooting upward like a pair of rockets!

"""Waaaaghhh!!"""

"Try to stick together, you two!" shouted Red, a dimension-hopping veteran at this point. Then all three were sucked into the hole, course set for N'nabadu's dreamworld.

The trio tumbled through a starscape of meterorites, each of them clinging to the other two for dear life.

"Wh-where are we?!" cried Bisco.

"We're in subspace! The space between dimensions!" yelled Red. "Hey, Milo! Don't let go!"

"…"

"Red! Milo's out cold!!"

It seemed that while Bisco and Red were built of sturdier stuff, the strain of crossing dimensions was more than Milo could withstand. Bisco and Red sandwiched him between their bodies to prevent him from drifting away.

"Hey!" Bisco yelled. "Can we even make it when we're one man down?!"

"How am I supposed to know?! Just shut up and concentrate!!"

"Listen, Red, there's somethin' I gotta tell you."

At Bisco's uncharacteristic sincerity, Red clammed up and listened.

"The mushrooms in my blood are callin' to me. They're sayin' this'll be unlike any journey we've ever faced. It might even be our last."

The voice of the mushrooms spoke reason. Even if the two Biscos succeeded in their mission, they might never see their home dimension again.

"So, Red! I have a favor to ask!"

"I don't have to listen to anything you say!"

"Well, I'll say it anyway! If I… If I die out there, I want you…"

Bisco paused before continuing.

"I want you to use your powers…and absorb my soul!"

"What?!" Red's jade-green eyes flew wide. She couldn't believe the target of her hunt would present himself so willingly. "Do you even understand what you're sayin'?!"

"I hate to admit it, but your power's the real deal. With my soul backin' you up, there ain't no one who can beat you! The whole world'll be safe with you watchin' over it. And so will Sugar and Salt…"

In a situation where all three were about to die, Bisco was willing to hand over his soul to Red. The future of the world and the safety of his children meant more to him than his own life. It was proof he had become a father at last.

"You can't be serious…"

"You get what I'm askin', right?" said Bisco. "I ain't givin' my soul away for free."

"I know. You don't have to say it." The expression on Red's face turned into a gentle smile. "You and I think the same way. You want me to look after your family in return, right?"

"Then it's a deal?"

Red stared into Bisco's eyes, a reflection of her own, as a long silence reigned. Then, at last, she bared her canines and grinned.

"It's a deal, Bisco!"

"Wargh!" cried Bisco as Red hooked a meaty arm around him, pulling him in.

"I promise!" she said. "So let me know now where you want your tattoo to be! I've still got space on my tongue, see?"

"And have to see the crap *you* eat? Blech, no thanks."

Chomp!

"Gaaagh!!"

"Well, look at that." Red grinned. "Guess I *do* eat crap! Ah-ha-ha-ha!"

The female Man-Eating Redcap went for his nose, and Bisco squealed in pain. With him rubbing his nose in agony, and with Milo passed out, there was no one to hear her next words.

"There's no doubt about it," she said to herself. "This guy's just as much Bisco Akaboshi as I am!!"

All the doubt and fear had vanished from her face. Red brimmed with vitality, and the tattoos across her body flared to life, propelling her onward through the mystical space.

8

A clap of thunder shook the heavens, and a flash of lightning lit up the holy city. Cold, hard rain battered the streets that weaved among and between towering pillars.

Aside from the storm, the night was eerily quiet. It was as if the whole town cowered before an angry god, eager to make their repentance known.

These were the Hundred-and-Eight Towers of Izumo.

After the Rust Lord bested Akaboshi in divine combat, none were left to stop him from conquering all of Japan. Izumo stood now as the nation's capital, and its hundred and eight faiths warred endlessly, sacrificing the laymen in tribute to their one and only god…

…or at least, such is the false history upon which this world is based.

Second mightiest of all the sects were the Flamebound. Their leader, Kyurumon, stood by the window, her keen and piercing eyes trained on the lightning outside.

I do not like it, she thought. *Even in a world of pure fiction, I am stuck as the leader of some worthless faith!*

"Lady Kyurumon," came a voice. "We have enough prayers now to present to the Rust Lord."

A lady of the cloth, unwise to the troubles of her mistress, appeared by Kyurumon's side. In her hands was a cylindrical container filled with entrails. It was a Scripture, full to bursting with holy power, causing the mantras inscribed across its surface to glow.

Behind the priestess stood rows of laypeople, all chanting in unison, "*On/aspal/shad/karna*," offering their life force to the next Scripture in line.

"We have filled six of the Scriptures, thus completing our current quota," the priestess said. "At this rate, our sect shall surely be first in line for the Rust Lord's favor, as usual."

"Hmm."

Kyurumon snarled.

The Rust Lord! Bah! Ridiculous. He may have installed himself as the one and only divine being, but in the end, he's just another puppet being strung along by the god of Rust!

"Lady Kyurumon...?"

"Is something the matter?"

"Enough! If you fools are content to wallow in ignorance, then so be it. Leave me."

Kyurumon waved away the priestesses with a sour look on her face, and just then...

Boom! Boom! Kaboom!

...a string of explosions outside shook the whole tower. While the devout citizens were tossed this way and that by the rumbling, Kyurumon's followers formed up defensively around her.

""Lady Kyurumon!""

"What's going on...?!"

Kyurumon activated her three masks and prepared for a fight. Rushing to the window, she watched as a ball of light fell from the heavens like a meteor, penetrating one of the towers on its way down, and causing it to collapse. Before her very eyes, the object struck a second tower, and a third. Like the weapon of a vengeful god, the light reduced the towers to rubble one by one.

"It's a meteor!" yelled one of her followers. "It's destroying the city!"

"Look! Even the Water Tower has fallen!!"

The glass-walled structure shattered under impact, releasing a torrent of water into the streets below.

Could it be...?!

Watching the orange streak lay waste to the city, Kyurumon anxiously bit her thumb.

That's no meteor! she thought. *That glow is caused by the friction of traveling between worlds! Has something finally managed to enter the Svapna Akasha from outside?!*

"Does that mean that dastardly Hylmaleo is no more?" asked an excited follower. "Oh, joy! Another of our wicked foes has—"

"Stand aside, fools!"

The priestesses all fell to the floor in repentance. Kyurumon snapped her fingers, and one of them placed a crimson cloak around her shoulders. Her eyes burned with the flame of ambition, aware as she was that her fabricated life was about to be turned upside down.

"That meteor," she said, "is an omen of ill that appears only once in ten thousand years. I must be by the Rust Lord's side in this trying time."

"Lady Kyurumon, you're going alone?!"

"Let us travel with you and—"

"You shall only hinder us. Remain here and strengthen our prayers."

The nuns all snapped to attention, while Kyurumon boldly leaped from the windowsill. Her pierced, bloodred lips formed a defiant grin, and even the masks swirling around her head seemed to move faster with the determination of their mistress.

Now is my chance!
I shall not rot to dust in this world of lies.
I shall seize this opportunity and return to the world where I belong!

* * *

The Rust Tower, the heart of Izumo's one hundred and eight towers. It was here, at the structure's base, that the orange meteor fell. The air was filled with the blaring of emergency sirens and the voices of panicking citizens.

...Gasp!!

Red shot awake at the pounding of her own heart. It seemed to have stopped beating and only now had restarted. The strain of crossing dimensions was great, but Red was somewhat used to it by now, and she made it through shaken but unharmed.

The spell must have worked, but I guess I'm trapped…

She recalled the sensation of colliding with something hard, and now she felt its weight pressing down on her. It seemed likely she was pinned under some rubble or suchlike.

Right, first job is to get outta here…huh?

Her hand fell upon something soft and smooth. Then she realized the pressure on her lips, and she finally opened her eyes.

Wh-wh-wh-whaaaat?!

The sight caused her blood to race!

Milo?!

What Red was pinned under wasn't rubble at all but Milo Nekoyanagi himself! And to make matters worse…

O-o-our lips, they're…touching!!

He was in the process of kissing her deeply!

"Mmmmmph!!" Red flailed.

"*Phah!* Red, are you—?"

"Paws off!!"

Thump!

"Guph?!?!"

Red unleashed a clothesline swing that caught Milo's neck, causing him to do a septuple backward somersault before colliding headfirst with the ground! Meanwhile, Red, in stark opposition to the brave warrior woman she had seemed…

"Waaaaah!!"

…sat on the floor and cried like a little girl.

"*Sob… Sob…* You kissed me!" she bawled. "How am I going to explain this to Pawoo?!"

"I-it's okay, Red... I... *Cough...!*"

"Oh no! I just felt a kick! Our second kid's on the way!!"

"No, they're not!! Calm down, Red, please!!" Hacking up blood, Milo struggled to his feet. "You passed out after we arrived! I was just performing CPR! I have a license to practice medicine, so don't worry, it's all aboveboard!"

"C-CPR...??"

"Pawoo will understand! So take deep breaths, okay?"

Milo hadn't expected Red to freak out to quite such an extent, but when he thought of Bisco's oft-surprising boyish innocence, it began to make sense. As Red calmed down, she seemed to grow embarrassed at her outburst, and even putting on a fearsome scowl couldn't hide the blood rushing to her cheeks.

"S-so what you're saying is...that doesn't count, from an ethical perspective...?"

"That's right! It was a lifesaving procedure, that's all!"

"Th-then I guess...we're good..."

Red covered her mouth with her cloak and drooped her head, casting Milo a reproachful glare. The boy doctor seemed completely guiltless, only smiling sweetly in the face of Red's defeat.

I—I messed up! she thought, growling with rage. *How could I let him pull one over on me?!*

Despite her embarrassment, Red knew it would be unbecoming to throw a fit. Instead...

"H...heh-heh! Still, I thought you might be good with the ladies, but I guess this world's Milo just ain't all that after all!"

Red folded her arms and puffed up her chest in order to cow the light world Milo into submission.

"I mean, you call that a real kiss?" she said. "You'll never please a girl with something like that!"

"In that case..."

Milo's face appeared right in front of hers.

"Do you want to try a real one?"

"Um—"

He was far too close for comfort. Red stared into his big round eyes, narrowed in a sultry way she had never seen on him before. He was like a hunter, a carnivore eyeing his prey, and Red's feigned courage fell apart like soggy paper.

"What's the matter, cold feet?" whispered Milo. "Don't start what you can't finish."

"Erm…! Um…! M-Milo! Wait, I was kidding!"

"Too late. You're not getting away. This is the perfect chance to teach you a lesson."

"Wh-wh-wh-whawhawhawha…!!"

The legendary Twinshroom, the dark world's strongest Mushroom Keeper, was at that moment so terrified that she couldn't speak a single word.

I-is this what Milo would be like as a boy?! Th-th-this can't be happening to me!!

Red closed her eyes, resigning herself to her fate, but at that moment…

"hellooo? are you two okay?"

"Oh! Bisco!"

Milo perked up and turned around to face the source.

"That's Bisco's voice, Red! Biscooo! We're over heeere!!"

Despite the faint and muffled quality of the voice, Milo recognized it instantly. But while he started shouting back to establish their position, Red was left with a distinct feeling of disappointment.

"H-huh?" she stammered. "Is that it?"

"Come now, Red. You can't be fooling around behind Blue's back!" Milo warned her. "If we'd kissed then, that definitely would have counted from an ethical perspective!"

"Y-you…you were playing tricks on me!"

"I can only imagine what Blue has to go through." Milo sighed. "Protecting you from untoward advances; I have to do the same thing with Bisco all the time! Listen here, Red; there are all sorts of dangerous men in this world. You have to learn how to say no!"

"*You're the most dangerous of them all!!*"...was what Red wanted to say, but Milo tugged her by the arm and urged her on toward Bisco's voice.

I can't believe this man! she thought. *Only Milo's allowed to play with my heart like that! ...Huh? Wait... I guess he is Milo...*

Red contended with this realization in her head as she followed Milo.

* * *

It soon became clear that the three of them had landed halfway up a large tower, and the view from the windows revealed the rain-stricken cityscape of Izumo. The city looked much as Milo remembered it, only far larger, and the streets stretched out in all directions as far as the eye could see.

"Looks like we're in a version of Japan that fell to the Rust Lord faith," said Red.

"Yeah. I guess N'nabadu made it this way to remove me and Bisco. This is what the world would have looked like if we'd never beaten Kelshinha..."

"Pathetic. How could you lose to that old man?"

"We didn't! That's what I'm saying! This is an alternate reality where—!"

"hellooo?"

A tiny voice.

"Bisco! Where are you?!"

Milo looked around. He and Red were in a large, mosque-like building with a high roof, but try as he might, he couldn't spot Bisco anywhere.

"i'm right here."

"Right where?!"

"This ain't the time for hide-and-seek!" yelled Red. "Come out here, now!"

"i'm right here, assholes! right in front of you!"

"""What?!"""

The two cast a nervous glance at each other, then slowly, they craned their necks toward the altar, from where the voice issued.

"here i am."

Standing atop it was a cute little mushroom man, with big googly eyes and a somewhat vexed expression. A pair of boots and gloves snugly covered his chunky hands and feet, while a cloak and bow sat atop his back. It was as if someone had dressed up a mushroom in the garb of a Mushroom Keeper.

"What the hell is that?!" screamed Red, her eyes wide. "It's a *zashiki-warashi* on shrooms!"

"no, it's me!"

"B-Bisco?! You got turned into a monstroom!"

Even Milo couldn't hold in his surprise. He examined the fungal homunculus from every angle, but there was no denying the short-statured shroom was his very own partner.

"How did this happen to you, Bisco?! What do you remember?!"

"well, you passed out when we were movin' between dimensions, and i had to take the strain for the two of us. then it looks like my body entered some kind of 'safe mode'..."

Bisco appeared quite angered by this development and cried out at the top of his lungs. However, given his miniature size, this only caused him to sound about average.

"i figure it'll heal on its own," he said. *"let's forget about it. everyone's here now, so let's get movin', people!"*

I don't think you count as people... thought Red.

S-so cute...

"don't look at me like that. i may be a mushroom now, but i'm still the same bisco akaboshi you all know and love. watch this."

The mushroom-morphed Bisco stuck out his chest and flexed his little arms, and just like with a cartoon character, small bumps appeared on his biceps. This was finally too much for Milo, who screamed "Cuuuute!!" and picked up Bisco in his fingers. Bisco struggled to no avail, his stumpy little legs flailing in the air while he dangled before Milo's eyes.

"put me down!"

"I can't! You're too cute! Coochie-coochie-coo!"

"ah-ha-ha-ha-ha!"

Milo may have only been playing with him, but to Bisco, this was a matter of life and death. The spores surged to protect him, building up energy in his eyes.

"take this! mushroom beam!!"

A jade-green light flew from Bisco's glare, knocking Milo in the face and deflecting his head upward. Bisco seized the opportunity to free himself from Milo's overly curious grasp and perched himself on Red's head, slipping underneath her cat-eye goggles.

"Whoa?!"

"lemme hang out here for a bit."

"Hey! What's the big idea, enterin' a lady's hair without askin'?!"

"you gotta look after number one, right? and since you and i are the same, you gotta look after me! we ain't got time to play around. we gotta hurry up and destroy this dimension before it destroys ours!"

"Aww, can't we just play around a *little* bit more?" Milo whined.

"the fate of the world's at stake!!"

Red was already tired of the two boys' bickering and was ready to accept whatever it would take to shut them up, when all of a sudden...

"On/shad/libtoreo/snew!!"

"!!"

A whirlpool of gold appeared underfoot, which rose into a tornado and tried to tear the three apart! Red swiftly hooked Milo under her arm and leaped out of it, becoming covered in gold dust but emerging safely on the chapel floor.

"This is chrysokinesis—gold manipulation!"

"Bah-hah-hah-hah! See, Kyurumon? It is just as the Rust Lord revealed to us!"

"Do not laugh as your prey eludes you, dullard. I should have known better than to rely on you for this task."

Milo and Red both turned to see a morbidly obese gentleman wearing an opulent robe and, behind him, a stunningly beautiful woman dressed in crimson.

"Corpulo of the Gilded Elephants…and Kyurumon of the Flamebound!!" cried Milo.

"who were they again?"

While Bisco tilted his mushroom head in confusion, Corpulo licked his lips, like a wild boar spotting its next meal.

"The evil spirit Akaboshi, and Nekoyanagi, his familiar! Once those two are out of the picture, this false world—the Svapna Akasha—will overwrite the light world and become our true reality! Or at least… that *is* what we were promised, is it not, Kyurumon?"

"Doubt is blasphemy, pig. Shut your mouth and let your actions do the talking."

"*Snork! Snork! Snork!* It has been a while since I last stretched my legs, but I will do whatever it takes to become real again! In the name of the Gilded Elephants, I shall offer up your head to the Rust Lord!"

"these guys know they're just fakes!"

"Then why don't you just stand aside and make way for some real ones, fatty?" said Red, her courageous voice scattering the gold dust in the halls. "It doesn't matter how real you are—it won't stop you from livin' fake-ass lives!"

"Heh-heh-heh. You hear that, Corpulo? The red one has your number, it seems."

Kyurumon laughed in response to Red's cutting jest, but…

"Snork! Snork! Snooorkkk…!!"

Her words put Corpulo on the warpath! Perhaps realizing it was not prudent to stir up her own ally, Kyurumon patted his bald head and said, "There, there. Settle down. That arrogant woman appears to be the dark world's Akaboshi. Look closely at her. Doesn't she have a lot of meat on her bones, just the way you like them?"

"Snork?"

Now that she mentioned it, while Red's marvelous muscles were the first thing many noticed about her, Corpulo's discerning eye was not blind to the beautiful structure of her facial features, either.

"Our god never said anything about her," said Kyurumon. "I'll tell you what—once we finish exterminating the other two, you can have her."

"Y-you're giving her to me?! *Snork! Snork! Snork!*"

With a disgusting laugh and equally disgusting grin, Corpulo began shuffling over toward Red.

"Bah-hah-hah! Rejoice, girl! You'll get to live…as my concubine!"

"You scumbag!"

The blood rose to Red's head, but before she could do anything, an arrow flew past her eyes and skewered the fat man's throat! The incredible force of its draw meant that it kept on going, lifting its overweight target clean off the ground, and before Corpulo could even work out what had happened, he was thrown out of a nearby window.

"Don't you dare say such disgusting things to Bisco."

It was Milo who had fired the blindingly fast arrow that sealed Corpulo's fate. His reactions had been immediate—the speed of a flash freeze—before Red's fire could even get going.

"Did you have enough time to regret it? …I guess not."

Red stood slack-jawed, her anger having nowhere to go and steadily being replaced with a trembling fear. Milo turned back to her and, with a smile, said, "All gone! He won't be talking now!"

scary, right?

Yeah… Much scarier than my Milo…

"Ah-ha-ha-ha-ha! Skewered like a pig! What a *boar*ish way to go!"

Kyurumon, on the other hand, seemed mostly unperturbed by the sudden removal of her ally, and instead let out a sharp chuckle that shocked the other three. She peered out the window to see that her anger mask had caught the man before he fell to his death.

"S-snork… Snorkkk… Kyurumon, you vixen! Bring me back up!"

Clutching his injured throat with one hand, he watched as Kyurumon floated before him.

"This was your purpose from the very beginning," she said.
"Snork?"
"What's that woman up to?" cried Red.
"hey, look at that!"
"On-shandreber-libtoreo-snew...!!"
As Kyurumon chanted her mantra, Corpulo's leaking blood turned into gold dust, forming a golden waterfall in midair.
"Huh?!" The schism between the two high priests threw Red for a loop. "What the hell is that?!"
"it's just a waterfall of gold. they're common in our world. guess a country bumpkin like you hasn't seen them before."
"I—I have, too!"
"Cut it out, you two! Look at what's happening outside!!"
Kyurumon's mantra was attracting the greedy citizens below. They scrambled over one another, linking themselves together in a large pile, like a great wave crashing against the walls! It wasn't long before Corpulo himself was swallowed up by the crowd.
""""Wh-what the—?!""""
"Ah-ha-ha-ha!!"
But the wave didn't subside there. It continued growing, drawing more and more people into its agglutinate mass, until it formed a giant humanoid figure!
"This is the culmination of Izumo's faith!" howled Kyurumon. "The Great Flesh Goddess Idol!"
""Flesh Goddess??""
"Strike them down!"
"uh-oh! outta the way, milo!!"
The divine incarnation swung a fist, crashing through the tower wall, but the three Mushroom Keepers had already evacuated into the night. Several greedy citizens lost their grip and fell from the amalgam's fist into the darkness below, while Red landed atop a different tower. Looking up at the form of the figure, she clicked her tongue.
"Red, let's come up with a plan!" shouted Milo.
"Don't need one...!"

Red drew her bow, affixed an arrow from her quiver to the string, and pulled it back. As she did, the tattoos across her body glowed with anticipation, emitting a burning heat.

"A few thousand people ain't chicken scratch compared to me. I'll just keep firing until they all go down."

"hey! listen to milo, will you?!"

"Take this!!"

Thud! Gaboom!

Red's arrows landed in the meat golem's thigh, chest, and arm in quick succession, giving rise to gigantic mushrooms.

W-wow!

Red's arrow was just a normal red oyster mushroom, but its power surpassed even that of Bisco's Rust-Eater. While Milo reeled in shock, Red's arrows blew bits off the Flesh Goddess Idol, causing it to temporarily fall still. However…

"Don't waste your time," said Kyurumon, sneering. "There are always more in Izumo willing to sell their souls for money!" She recited her gold-spawning mantra once more, and sure enough, another couple hundred people scaled the meat giant to restore its wounded parts.

"Tch…"

"That's why I said to come up with a plan, Red!" cried Milo. "She can just heal any damage we do right away!"

"Then I'll just keep shootin' until there's no one left!"

"You'll kill everyone in the city!"

"Damn right! Got a problem with that?!"

Red spun to face Milo, her hair fluttering and sweat flying, and stared directly into his starlight eyes.

"It's a dog-eat-dog world, Milo. You have to take what you can, before everything that's yours is taken away from you! So you can either stand there and watch, or you can help me out!"

"Red…!"

"Strike them down, my fools!!"

"Dammit!!"

At Kyurumon's order, citizens began gathering at the Flesh Goddess's index finger, forming a whip of bodies that lashed out at the three Mushroom Keepers. Red tried to flee, but Kyurumon's creation relentlessly followed, toppling several towers in its path.

I see now, thought Milo. *She's what Bisco could have ended up like. She's had to bear it all by herself, and now she thinks that in order to protect something, you have to kill something!*

"milo!"

Who should come flying in and strike Milo's furrowed brow but the fungified Bisco?! He desperately clawed at Milo's hair, clutching a few sky-blue strands so he didn't fall.

"what's wrong with you? come up with a plan like you always do!"

"I have a plan, Bisco! But Red's not listening to me! What should I do?"

"well, that's 'cause you ain't her partner yet."

"What does that mean?!"

"you gotta call her by name!" yelled Bisco, slapping Milo's scalp with his shrunken hands. *"she might be powerful, but as long as she's 'red,' she's all alone. you gotta be her partner—her milo, and call her by name!"*

"...Okay, got it!" came Milo's swift comprehension. "But wait... Doesn't that mean I'll be cheating on you?"

"uhh, what?"

"I'm saying...even if it's only for a bit, I'll be acting as someone else's partner. Are you really okay with that?"

"what are you talkin' about?! just do it already!"

Meanwhile, Red battled the Flesh Goddess. "This regeneration is pissin' me off!" she growled. "Try this on for size!!"

She grabbed a silveracid *nameko* arrow from her quiver and pulled back, loading the arrow with enough force to reduce the whole city to rubble.

"Dieeeeee—!"

"Bisco, wait!!"

"!!"

Somehow, Red knew he was calling her. Milo's voice was filled with so much love and trust that it couldn't have been anyone else.

"M-Milo?!"

Her hand stopped. She could feel Blue's presence in his words. She knew that if she just trusted him, everything would be okay. She gave herself over to the feeling.

"Bisco! Trust my plan!"

"Wh-why are you calling me that?!"

"Just pretend I'm Blue for now. Milo would never lead you astray, right?"

A look of calm slowly spread across Red's—across *Bisco's*—face. With her partner's warmth permeating her body, she felt her worries melt away.

Why…why am I such a pushover?!

As the power welled up inside her, Red felt a taste of bitterness, too.

All he did was say my name! Dammit!

"What are you waiting for?! Smite her!!"

Sensing the tables were about to turn, Kyurumon ordered her construct to finish Red off. However, Milo leaped in at the last second with a mantra barrier that kept Red safe.

"You listened!" he said, sidling over to her. Then, whispering in her ear, "Hey, how would you say I measure up to Blue?"

"Th-that feels weird, cut it out. Stop messin' with me!"

"We'll need the Jizou mushroom. Do you have one?"

"Jabi's invention?!" Red had been curious to hear Milo's plan, but this was far from what she expected. "But all that does is turn into a statue! How's that gonna help us?"

"No time to explain! Do you have one or not?"

"I—I guess I can get one from Jabi's tattoo. Rrrrgggghhh…! Here it comes…!!"

Red focused on the tattoo covering her upper arm, and in her hand materialized an arrow she thought she'd never use in combat.

Then Milo summoned the Mantra Bow and handed it to Red. She nocked the arrow, and it glowed with an emerald light. Red nodded once, then pulled the bowstring tight.

"Ready to go, Milo!"

"All right!"

""Mantra Jizou Arrow!!""

Twang!!

"Fools!"

Kyurumon swiftly stepped in, manipulating her masks to protect the golem…but it seemed that was not the arrow's target. Instead, it landed in the ground several meters ahead. And then…

Gaboom!!

"Wh-wh-what in the Six Realms is that?!"

What appeared was not a mere roadside Jizou, as expected. The Mantra Bow had amplified the arrow's power, causing it to birth an enormous mushroom re-creation of the Buddha himself, a benevolent smile upon his lips and his hands arranged in a religious gesture.

"It worked! We created the Great Spore God!"

"The *what*?!"

Even Red, the statue's creator, couldn't work out what had just happened. But mysteriously, though the statue was doing nothing at all, the Flesh Goddess halted upon seeing it.

"Wh-what are you waiting for?!" shrieked Kyurumon. "Flatten that ugly thing!"

As she was trying in vain to get her amalgam to move, Bisco hopped atop the statue's head and, using a handy loudshroom, made an air-shaking announcement.

"THOU GAZETH UPON THE FORM OF THE GREAT SPORE GOD (God) (god…)."

"Th-the Great Spore God?!"

"THOU SHALT NEVER REACHETH SALVATION IFETH THOU TURNETH FROM REALITY TO GOLD AND MONEY. IFETH THOU WISHETH TO FIND HAPPINESS IN THIS LIFE, THOU MUSTETH TREASURE LIFE AND FAMILY (Family) (family…)."

"Are you kidding me?!" Kyurumon snarled. "Take that thing out already! Can't you hear me?!"

But…

"...Whoa..."

"Praise be!"

"Life *is* more important than money!"

"I'm going home right now!"

Almost immediately, the teachings of the Great Spore God broke each and every citizen out of their stupor. They ran back to their families, causing the golem to grow smaller and smaller.

"H-h-h-how could this happen?!"

In the end, Corpulo was all that remained. His wounds apparently healed, the obese head priest jolted awake...and immediately got on his hands and knees in prayer.

"O Great Spore God..."

"You fat oaf! Curse it! Curse it all!"

Kyurumon went rosy-cheeked with indignation, planted her foot upon Corpulo's backside, and dragged him away by the scruff into the dark streets of Izumo.

"You'll pay for this, demons!" she howled. "You haven't seen the last of me!"

* * *

"..."

From atop the statue's shoulders, Red peered down at the city. She had just witnessed something she couldn't laugh off. Milo and Bisco's teamwork had not just defeated their foe—it had awoken the good living inside the hearts of men and ended the battle without violence.

Is this what Jabi wanted? she pondered.

Her teacher had always said that the greatest battles were won without shooting a single arrow.

...Ridiculous!

Red ground her teeth, refusing to accept this victory. Jabi's teachings flew in the face of her own personal philosophy.

How are you supposed to find faith in your foe when it's a fight to the death?! The only way to claim victory is to tear it from their cold, dead hands!

However, whether knowledgeable or not about the conflict brewing in Red's mind, Bisco hopped down from the statue's head and placed his chin thoughtfully in his hands.

"*i get it now,*" he said. *"this is why jabi invented the jizou mushroom: to build his foes up instead of tearin' 'em down. that was his dream."*

"A childish dream! You can't let your foes live and call it victory! Jabi was foolish to believe that!"

From Red's perspective, nothing had been won. If you won, you killed. If you lost, you died. That was the rule in the cold, harsh world where she grew up.

"maybe so. but it came true."

"...Grh... That was just...!!"

"or maybe it didn't. but who cares?"

Bisco sat on Red's shoulder and spoke, his words gently seeping into Red's unsettled heart.

"it don't matter if it came true or not, 'cause that ain't why we dream. the journey itself is the dream; that's what livin's all about."

Red gasped. Bisco's words had shaken her philosophy to its core. Was he saying that instead of accepting reality as it was, it was better to dream?

"You're wrong!!"

"huh?! whoa!"

She couldn't accept it! Overcome by a mysterious rage, she grabbed Bisco and held him in front of her. Her eyes quivered in time with her wavering heart.

"You got lucky! It was a fluke! Don't act like you've solved all of life's problems! You just happened to come out on top! That's why Pawoo and Tirol and Actagawa are all still with you!!"

"y-you're squashing me... stop..."

"If it was that easy to save them, then why...? Why couldn't I...?!"

"Bisco!!"

Red dropped Bisco and turned away just as Milo hopped nimbly through the night to rejoin them. Seeing the somewhat sullen pair, Milo looked first at Red, then at Bisco, then nodded.

"Red's been crying," he surmised. "What did you do to her, Bisco?!"

"whaaat?! i didn't do nothin'!"

"You'll get a tickling."

"why?!"

"I've figured out where the Rust Lord is," said Milo, swiftly changing the subject. "Given that the Rust Lord faith is dominant in this world, it stands to reason that the Rust Lord himself must be the master. If we take him down, this world should vanish!"

"so we just gotta go for round two with this Kelshinha dude, huh? seems easy enough to me! i'll show him what a good father looks like!"

"Not at that size, you won't," said Milo. "Better leave this to me. Mama knows best!"

"you take that back!!"

"Come on, you two! Follow me!"

Milo leaped from the statue, and Red followed, Bisco clinging to her brow. She spoke so that only he could hear.

"...Bisco, I respect your journey as much as anyone's, but there's one thing you ought to know."

"hmm?"

"You're only safe to dream because you're held up by those who see the truth. If you don't shoot your arrows or spill your enemies' blood, then someone else will do it for you."

"..."

"You're allowed to do that, but don't you dare look down on me. I'm just the only one around here who's willing to get my hands wet."

Even if Bisco could have formulated a response, Red would not listen. She pulled down her cat-eye goggles and hid her face from the night.

9

Click.

Click. Click.

The sound of a lock being picked.

A single man, frail as a withered tree and dripping with sweat, fought with the lock hanging from a display case.

*"On...kel...shad...*pant...pant...*on...kel...shad...snew..."*

It was clear the old man was not much longer for this world. He was all skin and bones, and he was in such a great panic that it seemed unlikely he had any more sweat to lose.

"I...just need...the Scriptures..."

His voice sounded like sandpaper in his throat.

"I...just need...my organs back...!"

If the man had possessed his former drive and ambition, nobody would have failed to recognize his bloodshot eyes and hawklike nose. Nobody would have failed to realize that this was Lord Kelshinha himself, the man who had once ruled Izumo with an iron fist.

But what had become of him now? He was not the superman of magic and muscle that Bisco had fought in the past. If anything, he looked exactly like when the pair had first picked him up in the dungeons of the bandit castle.

"On/kel/shad/rin/kel/shad! How dare you...? How dare you usurp my throne, you brat?! The Scriptures are mine! I'll...I'll..."

Click!

"Yes! It's open!"

With gleeful eyes, Kelshinha removed the lock and extended his trembling hands toward the case. As he opened the doors, it exuded a chill wind, for this case contained several cylinders, each preserved in a refrigerated state. They were, indeed...

"The Scriptures...!"

Kelshinha's five organs, each imbued with mantra power.

"Yesss! Once I have these back, I can..."

Kelshinha reached inside the case and laid his hands on one of the cylinders! But just as he was about to slide it out...

"What?! M-my fingers!"

Kelshinha watched as his fingers immediately began disintegrating into Rust. The frightful sight caused him to fall over backward and stare at his hand in horror.

"Aghh! My hand! It's rusting! Aaaaaghh!!"

"Hyuk, hyuk, hyuk..."

Someone was standing in the doorway, laughing at him. It was a young man with long fluffy hair that fell down to his waist and thin, mysterious eyes, as well as a strange, feminine beauty.

He was Amli, the Rust Lord, the true master of this false world.

"Too much mischief, and the god's wrath will come down on you." The boy chuckled. *"Did you not teach as much yourself, Father?"*

"Y-you rotten worm!" Kelshinha clutched his disintegrating arm, turning his sweat-stained face on Amli. "Undo this mantra at once! I'm dying!"

"*What an awful name to call your own son,*" Amli replied. *"What am I to think of that? Perhaps the world would be better off without you."*

"P-please! Have mercy, O wise god! Show mercy to an old and feeble man!"

"Hyuk, hyuk—oops, I mean... Tee-hee."

Correcting his vulgar laugh, the young man snapped his fingers, and the disintegration stopped. Kelshinha stared at his missing hand and gave a long, shallow sigh, a mixture of relief and remorse.

"It is as you say, Father. Your son Amli is a good child, isn't he?"

"Curse you, insect… All you do is steal her power…"

"Oh? That isn't the response I wanted to hear."

"Th-thank you for your divine miracle, O great and powerful Rust Lord!!"

"Tee-hee-hee-hee! That's better. It's good to see you've lost that repugnant arrogance of yours."

The boy patted Kelshinha on his bald head and gave a gloating smile that only made Kelshinha tremble even more.

That was because he knew the boy before him was not his own child but the assassin N'nabadu, servant of the Rust god, a being so terrifying that all he could do was quiver.

"This is a world in which you defeated Akaboshi, Father. It's what you always wanted. Why are you still afraid?"

"B-but…," said Kelshinha between panicked breaths, "my desire was not simply to kill Akaboshi; it was to become the one true god. This fate is no different than death. What worth is victory if there is no power to enjoy it?"

Amli's face turned cold upon hearing those words. *"The one true god, you say? Pathetic. There can be only one god to rule over all of space-time, and that is my Lord Rust. He has power you could never even dream of."*

"Urgh…!!"

"Hyuk, hyuk, hyuk! Rest assured, Father, you will be allowed to live out your few remaining years in peace…as a servant of Lord Rust! …Oh, look, you've left the Scriptures lying around again…"

Amli picked up the fallen cylinder and replaced it inside the case, locking the door in full view of the horrified Kelshinha.

The godhood I fought for…was it really not meant to be mine? That… that cannot be! If only I had his body…! If only I had the protection of his god!!

* * *

Kelshinha's eyes shot open, and he yelled.

"Give me your body, N'nabadu!!"

He scooped a glass shard off the floor and launched it at Amli while his back was turned!

But...

"Completely unrepentant..."

Muttering a curse under his breath, Amli swiveled around and, with sharpened nails like knives, left four bloody cuts across Kelshinha's face.

"Gaagh!!"

"Why can you not be satisfied with this false reality, you miserable old man?"

Amli turned to look at Kelshinha and the blood streaming down his face, and he raised a single finger. Particles of Rust began gathering in it, forming the shape of a cogwheel, which spun fast enough to tear the old man to mincemeat.

"I thought it would at least be useful to keep you alive, but I guess not. Seeing you will only depress my lord further. I shall deal with you here and now."

"Eee!!"

"I will grind your meat and your soul into space-time dust!"

"Eeee!!"

But just as the wicked old man was about to meet a grisly fate...

Shwf!

Kroom!!

...Red's arrow smashed the spinning cogwheel to pieces, then landed on the ground between Amli and Kelshinha, before exploding with a *Gaboom!* and launching the old man away!

"What's happeniiing?!"

"Hold on!"

Milo caught the falling Kelshinha and brought him back to the room he was in—the top of the Rust Tower, the Rust Lord's private quarters. After putting him down, both Red and Milo stood in front of him and stared at Amli, who was floating gently in midair.

"Milo, who's the old man?"

"It's Kelshinha. He's about to die!"

"Ugh…"

"*wh-what the hell?!*" yelled Bisco, looking down from Milo's head at the emaciated old man—the very figure he thought was the cause of this whole mess. "*i thought we were here to kill the rust lord, but it looks like he don't need our help!*"

"Ah, if it isn't the jolly light world gang."

Amli gave a bewitching smile. Spinning cogwheels hung in the air around him, forbidding anyone from coming close.

"And you, Sister. It's been a while."

"did he just call you 'sister'?"

"Amli!!"

Bisco wasn't sure what he was seeing, but Red's face immediately curled up with rage, seeing the figure of the friend she had fought alongside in the past.

"No, you're not Amli. It's N'nabadu, ain't it? Using his body like the freak you are. Speaking with his voice!!"

"And whatever is wrong with that?" the boy replied. *"Am I not allowed to use my own voice?"*

"Quit messing around! Amli's—"

"—Dead."

Red's words stopped in her throat, while the boy—or to use his true name, N'nabadu—adopted a gleeful grin.

"Yes he is. He gave his life for you, and Lord Rust gobbled him up. Do you remember how he screamed, bloodied and broken?"

"Stop it…"

"How sad. All of them had a reason to live, even this one. And yet they all had to die, because of you."

"Stop it! Shut up!!"

"Hyuk! Hyuk, hyuk, hyuk!!"

N'nabadu jabbed his finger in Red's face and laughed, spitting on the boy's sacrifice while wearing his very skin.

"Oh, I do so love toying with you, Mushroom Keeper. It never gets old."

Just as Red seemed about to lose it to his taunts, Milo and Bisco stepped forward.

"What a cruel being! Keep it together, Red!"

"yeah. i mean, that don't even look like amli. if you look closely, you can tell he's a boy!"

"Yeah, but from Red's point of view, that *is* the real Amli. Don't you remember? In the dark world, everyone's gender is swapped."

"whaat?! but this guy's even taller than me!"

"I think all of humanity is taller than you at this point, Bisco."

"asshole. you think that's funny?"

"I'm just stating facts."

"your eyelashes are gonna get it."

"Agh! Stop pulling on them!!"

"Shut the hell up, you two!"

At long last, Red lost her temper and screamed. There wasn't time to worry about whatever nonsense the two boys were spouting this time.

"Can't you tell this is serious?!"

"he started it."

"No, he did!"

"Shut up and listen!!"

"Sorry!"

"sorry!"

Usually, Red would have given herself over to the will of her burning tattoos, but this time, she found that the boys' pointless quarrel had allayed her anger and staved off despair in their place.

". . . Tch."

N'nabadu, on the other hand, was annoyed that his taunting hadn't had the usual desired effect, and he turned his attention to Bisco and Milo.

". . . So you've come to oppose me, too? The light world versions of Red and Blue? You don't even have the power that Red has; how are you ever going to stand against me?"

"We'll figure something out!"

"we always do!"

Bisco and Milo struck complementary poses, while Amli, growing increasingly frustrated, caused his aura to flare.

"You just couldn't sit tight and wait for this world to end, could you? Very well. If you yearn for oblivion so dearly, then I shall grant it to you!"

"Here he comes!"

"We're ready!"

"let's do this!"

"K-kill him!" screeched Kelshinha from behind the trio's backs. "I am the one true god! He is naught but a false blasphemy! Get rid of him, Nekoyanagi!!"

"glad to see the old man hasn't changed," said Bisco with a sigh, when...

Boom!

...Amli hurled a cogwheel chakram at Kelshinha's feet, destroying the floor and opening up an enormous hole! The old man fell through, plummeting to the lower levels with a rapidly fading squeal.

"Serves you right, you decrepit old fool."

"gramps!!"

"Leave him!" cried Red. "We have more important things to deal with!"

"i'll just be a sec!"

"What?! You're crazy! Get back here!"

Bisco leaped from Milo's brow and into the hole. Red was so shocked by his behavior that she didn't see Amli's attack coming until it was too late to react.

"Red, watch out! *Barrier!!*"

Milo threw up a mantra shield before grabbing Red's arm and leaping out of the tower. They both landed on the telegraph lines strung between the towers, with the nightscape of Izumo stretched out below.

"Keep it together, Red! Don't space out!"

"*You* try to keep your partner under control!" Red retorted. "Kelshinha was evil! Why is he wasting his effort tryin' to save him?!"

"I agree with you, Red. But Bisco's different."

"Then tell him—!!"

"I see. So even in the light world, Blue possesses no small measure of mantra power."

Amli alighted upon the wires without a sound, remaining a short distance above the duo, peering down on them mockingly.

"*However,*" he said. *"Compared to the Blue* I *know, your spells are like cheap conjurer's tricks."*

"What?!"

"You grew up in the tepid waters of the light world. You are still too green to adopt the name of Twinshroom. Too inexperienced to call yourself Red's partner."

"Hah! Let him keep running his mouth, Milo," said Red, finally readying herself for combat. "N'nabadu's a coward! All he can do is talk! All we gotta do is wait for our chance, and then…"

"What did you say…?"

"Huh?"

"Did you say…I'm not fit to be Bisco's partner…?!"

"Whaa?!"

N'nabadu had only meant to test the boy's temperament a little, but his taunts elicited a much greater reaction than expected. Even if she was from a different dimension, Red was still Bisco, and Milo's soul reacted before his mind could step in.

"How can you say that…when I've had one of his children?!"

Milo's mantra cube began spurting Rust, which formed into a giant battle-ax in Milo's hand. He leaped with unprecedented speed, and with uncanny strength, he swung the ax down on N'nabadu's head.

"Hah! So easily provoked. This barrier shall be enough to—"

"*President's Axe!!*"

Smash!!

Milo's attack blew the barrier to smithereens!

"What?! Grr…!!"

"You idiot! Cancel it, now!!"

"What strength. It's like he's a different person!!"

N'nabadu wiped the sweat from his brow. He couldn't believe the Milo standing before him was the same quiet boy from only a few moments ago.

"He's not like Blue at all. This Milo... is batshit crazy!!"

"Do you still think...?" Milo asked.

"Eep?!"

"Do you still think...I'm weaker than Blue?!"

Milo spun in a circle, transferring the energy of his revolution into the President's Axe once more! The impact slammed N'nabadu into the side of a nearby tower.

"...He may be strong, but he is easier to manipulate than Blue."

N'nabadu's wicked smile persisted in spite of his injuries. He readjusted Amli's garb and hopped back down onto the wires.

"I see I underestimated you," he said, adopting Amli's polite tone. *"But I am a mere servant of Lord Rust; a meager fly that Blue could have easily squashed without Red's help."*

"What?!"

"Don't listen to him, Milo! We have to work together!"

"Do you, now? So you do need to lean on Red after all. Drag them all down because you can't shine by yourself."

"Shut uuup!!"

Flames of anger burst to life in Milo's eyes, and an unparalleled torrent of power flowed into his cube. He raised his arm overhead and yelled...

"Come to me!!"

The Mantra Bow, glittering emerald, appeared in his hand without Bisco's assistance. Guided by fury, Milo drew back an arrow, while emerald spores poured forth, turning his hair green.

"I'll put a hole in you!!"

"Milo, stop!! You're showing the Rust god your full power!"

"Take this!! Mantra Bow!!"

Ka-chew!

Milo's arrow surpassed the speed of sound, with enough power to skewer N'nabadu in midair and choke the life out of him once and for all…

But!

"Hyuk, hyuk, hyuk…"

"""What?!"""

"Ah-hah-hah-hah!!"

The arrow hung, motionless, just millimeters from N'nabadu's breast, and with a sweep of his hand, he plucked it out of the sky.

"The Mantra Bow, you say? Ridiculous. Mantra is simply a means of controlling the Rust! All you are doing is borrowing my lord's power!!"

"What?!"

"You'll never lay a scratch on me…with such ancient technology!!"

With the Mantra Bow completely under his control, Amli swung his arm, and the arrow shot back at Milo, who had exhausted all his power on the attack and had nothing left with which to put up a barrier!

"Oh no!!"

"Dammit!!"

Red lunged into the arrow's path, ready to take the shot in Milo's place, but it was clear she wouldn't make it. The unreal speed of Milo's arrow was to be his own undoing.

"Milo!!"

Thud!!

"On-kel-shad-vakini."

"On-ul-kamlaitao-kelshinha-snew."

The arrow…hit something else!! A wall of meat and muscle suddenly leaped from the streets below, landing before Milo and taking the hit meant for him.

"""Whaat?!"""

"Khaa…"

The enormous figure pulled the Mantra Arrow from their flesh and, while it was still fresh with their blood...placed it into their mouth and swallowed it whole before giving off a loud burp.

"The arrow that once rent my flesh...to think it is no threat to me now."

"It-it's you!" Milo cried.

"You remember me? Then I shall grant you one last chance to kneel, Nekoyanagi."

Milo's eyes were as wide as plates when he saw who stood before him—and realized the true identity of the man who had just rescued him from certain death.

"Kneel before Kelshinha, the *true* Rust Lord!"

It was the mad monk himself! Power coursed through his flesh, and he looked just as healthy, if not *more* so, than when the boys had fought him at the height of his power.

"Did you see that, Red?!" Milo exclaimed. "Kelshinha just saved my life!!"

"He'd never do something like that. He's gotta be planning a trick!"

But Kelshinha ignored their conversation. Instead, he seemed to be talking to himself, angling his head down toward his own chest.

"I have upheld my end of the deal," he said. "My debt to you is paid, Akaboshi."

Upon closer examination, there was something golden and shining embedded in the pit of Kelshinha's stomach. And upon even *closer* examination, the thing appeared to be moving around as if alive.

"like hell it's paid! you've still gotta defeat that asshole, remember?!"

"Milo, look!"

"H-how did Bisco get there?!"

It wasn't clear how it had happened, but the mushroom-mode Bisco was embedded in Kelshinha's torso, right where N'nabadu's attack had left a hole in his flesh. It appeared Bisco himself was functioning as the mad monk's stomach, prolonging his life.

"Ridiculous. How long must I bow to the orders of my divine foe?

All of you will be dead soon enough, and I, Kelshinha, shall rule over all!"

"big talk for someone on a lifeline, old man. if you don't like our arrangement, then maybe I'll go take a walk!"

"Grh..."

"What is the meaning of this?!" N'nabadu roared, sweat beading on his brow. *"I thought I killed that old fool!!"*

Kelshinha turned to him and grinned. "Ha-ha-ha. That idiotic look suits you, despicable fly."

"How dare you...?!!"

N'nabadu had been enjoying grinding the old man underfoot and wasn't too happy to see the roles suddenly reversed.

"Who do you think you're talking to, you senile old rat?! I am the Rust god's right hand! You should be bowing to me! Revering me!"

"Do you know what the greatest sin in the universe is?" asked Kelshinha, laying a hand on Bisco and drawing the Rust-Eater's power into the form of a sunlight-colored spear. "It is blasphemy. The blasphemy to proclaim yourself a god before the one and only Rust Lord, Kelshinha! Now that I walk once more upon this Earth, all other gods, your master included, are naught but seatless pretenders!"

"D-damn you!! How dare you talk that way about Lord Rust?!"

"Run along, fly. Tell your master that I shall let him live...if he swears eternal fealty to me!!"

"Curse you!!"

Driven by rage, N'nabadu launched himself at Kelshinha, who readied his golden spear. The servant of the Rust god was consumed by a fury so great, the cogwheels spun fast enough to tear Amli's body apart.

"looks like a big one's comin', old man. you sure you can handle it?" asked Bisco.

"He may be a loathsome insect, but Amli's flesh is not to be underestimated. We must summon more strength, Akaboshi!"

"how about you stop rilin' him up for no reason?!"

"Dieee!!"

N'nabadu combined several cogwheels into a spinning lance and shot it toward Kelshinha. The two spears clashed in the night like fireworks.

"What?! How can a measly mantra spear hold up against my lord's cogwheels?!"

"Heh-heh-heh. This is no mantra spear, fly. This is the Rust-Eater, the mushroom of my sworn foe! It may be powerless against a true god such as myself, but it is more than suitable for dealing with pretenders like you!"

"it killed you, too, in case you forgot!"

"Hmph. It doesn't matter what powers you steal! You're a decrepit old fool, while my flesh is young and powerful! Let me show you!"

Just as N'nabadu said, Amli's life force was getting sucked out of her body and into the cogwheel lance, causing the wheels to spin even faster. Even the Rust-Eater spear was beginning to chip and wear under the constant clashes, and spores flew off it like sparks in the night.

"Hyuk, hyuk! Ha-ha-ha! You call yourself the Rust Lord?!" N'nabadu yelled. *"You're just a stinking human relying on Lord Rust's dregs!!"*

Mantra is merely a castoff of the Rust god's power... In that case, I shall go on searching...for a power to call my own!

"...Ohm yajur sama rig veda."

"whoa?!"

Bisco looked up at Kelshinha's face to see his eyes closed in concentration, his lips muttering some unknown spell. The words sounded unlike anything Bisco had ever heard Milo use.

"Ohm upani brihad aranyan."

"what are those, our last rites?! we can't give up now!"

"Ah-ha-ha-ha! What's the matter, old man, run out of false courage?!"

"Ohm brahma vishnu shiva."

N'nabadu chuckled at the sight of his foe abandoning victory and devoting himself to prayer. "*Perish before the might of Lord Rust!!*" he yelled, raising his lance and preparing to deliver the final blow!

"Raja vajra."

Clanggg!

"...What?!"

For an instant, N'nabadu was unable to decipher what had just happened. Then he realized: His lance was completely missing—along with the arm he had been using to hold it.

"M...my arm!!"

"whoa!!"

Something bright and golden like the sun had materialized behind Amli and sliced through his flesh! N'nabadu trembled with fear as he watched his own limb sail through the air.

"Raja vajra hanuman."

Splat! Splat!

The object danced to and fro, puncturing N'nabadu's body again and again. It was a *vajra*, formed of Rust-Eater power and guided by Kelshinha's spell to attack N'nabadu on its own.

"*Gaaaagh!!*" N'nabadu screamed. *"Th-this isn't mantra! You old fool, what have you done?!"*

The *vajra* returned to Kelshinha's side and floated, spinning, above his palm. The old man looked down at it and clicked his tongue.

"It is weaker than I expected," he said. "Only one in ten of the spores obey my words. The Rust was far easier to command, but the mushrooms, it seems, are a rebellious lot."

"*what the hell was that?!*" cried Bisco, unable to comprehend what he was seeing at first. From his position in the old man's chest, he had to crane his neck ninety degrees to look up at Kelshinha's face. *"the rust-eater must have accepted you! how the hell did you do it?"*

"The Rust and the mushrooms come from different mothers, but they are life all the same," Kelshinha replied. "As words control one, so do they control the other."

"the language of the mushrooms?! and you figured it out in just a few seconds?!"

"Who do you think you're talking to?" replied Kelshinha, cracking his neck and standing tall and proud. "I have always built up my power from nothing. I have always clawed my way back up when I am beaten. I am of a different breed from those who have carried their gifts from birth."

"Grrrrhhh!"

N'nabadu's eyes sparked with rage as he scrambled to heal the damage to Amli's body, but his flesh was cracked and unable to contain his own Rust power.

"This vessel can no longer support me! Is it because of my injuries?!"

"That vessel is my own flesh and blood, albeit of a different reality," answered Kelshinha. "It is too good for the likes of you."

"*yeah!*" shouted Bisco, and all of a sudden, a shining halo appeared at Kelshinha's back, the proof of his divine nature.

"For deceiving my child, you have incurred divine wrath. And I shall be the one to mete it out!"

"No…I need…a new vessel…"

On the verge of total bodily collapse, N'nabadu lunged!

"Give me yours!"

"now, old man!!"

"On-kel-shad-snew."

""Dadhichi Vajra!!""

Thus was forged an almighty combination attack between the Man-Eating Redcap and the Immortal Monk! The divine *vajra*, empowered by Bisco's Ultrafaith energy, tore a hole in N'nabadu's chest and engulfed him in golden flames.

"*Urgh… Ugh…*," he groaned, now a ball of fire illuminating the night. *"I'm burning… I'm burning… Oh, it burns… Grgghh…"*

"Heh-heh-heh. Hah-hah-hah-hah!!"

Kelshinha threw back his head and laughed, seeing his flames of purgatory eclipse the Rust god's power.

"This is most amusing, fly! Let me see you dance! Let me see you suffer!"

"cut it out, old man! the battle's won! finish him already!"

"Finish him?" Kelshinha looked down at Bisco and scoffed. "And why should I do that? This is the fate that awaits all those who blaspheme against me. Eternal damnation in a sea of flames!"

"y-you're insane!" Bisco yelled, but upon reflection, he realized he should have expected as much from the mad monk of Izumo. He began beating his stubby arms against Kelshinha's muscular chest, urging him to change his ways.

"you gotta show respect to your enemies, especially when they're dyin'! otherwise you're gonna make an enemy outta me!"

Kelshinha bent over and grinned a broad, teeth-revealing smile at the captive Bisco.

"Of you? Do my actions displease you? So what? Why should I be afraid of some miniature mushroom, Akaboshi?"

"grh...!"

"Heh-heh-heh! Remember, Akaboshi—after I destroy that fly, you are next! I shall scoop out your brain and make it mine for all eternity!"

"if that's the way you wanna play...! rgh! grgh! ...shit, i can't get out!"

Bisco wondered if it had perhaps been a mistake to share his power with Kelshinha, but it was too late now. His lower half was trapped inside Kelshinha's stomach cavity, and struggle as he might, he couldn't free himself—at least not before Kelshinha's hand came down on him!

"waah!!"

"Heh-heh-heh-heh—!"

Bwoom.

"—Hergh?!"

"huh?!"

Both Bisco and Kelshinha were equally surprised, for suddenly and without warning, the hand bearing down on Bisco completely disintegrated into nothing. It looked identical to what had happened to Bisco in the light world before.

"M-my arm!!"

"Hyuk, hyuk, hyuk! Ah-ha-ha-ha!"

Kelshinha spun around to see N'nabadu, still burning, laughing like a maniac. Amli's body had completely burned away, leaving only a squirming homunculus of Rust.

"You complete and utter fool, Kelshinha! Did you forget you're already dead in the real world?! Your continued existence is dependent on the Svapna Akasha, which I *maintain! Defeat me, and you cease to be!"*

"What...?!"

"What a joke! You're going to die by your own actions!!"

"That cannot be!! Aaargh!!"

"whoa?!"

Next, there was a *Shwompf!* and Kelshinha's abdomen vanished, dropping Bisco to the floor. Kelshinha, meanwhile, lost his balance, falling off the wires to the roof of the tower below.

"Y-you mean...?" he said through chattering teeth. "I am to die here, after I have perfected my ambition? After I have seized the throne of God with my own efforts, I am to die before anyone hears of my glory?"

"old man..."

"Not if I have anything to say about it, Kelshinha!"

Those spirited words came from the mouth of Bisco's parallel self, Twinshroom Red. She scooped Bisco off the floor and landed beside Kelshinha, carrying a grateful-looking Milo beneath her other arm.

"I saw how you dealt a blow against the Rust god just now. And I also happen to know of a way we can take you back to the real world!"

"What?!"

"Red, you don't mean...?!!"

"My Soul Absorption!" she exclaimed, indicating the tattoos across her face and neck. "If I absorb his soul, Kelshinha can go on living as a part of me. That includes all of his techniques and accomplishments!"

"you're gonna eat a guy like this? forget it!"

"Yeah, he'll give you a tummyache!"

But Kelshinha lowered his voice and muttered to himself.

"To live on...inside Akaboshi..."

He stared at his rapidly fading arm, then addressed Red.

"Very well," he said reluctantly. "Do it."

"Really?"

"I shall allow you to enshrine my perfect soul within that vessel of yours, Akaboshi. But know this! Should your power wane, I shall not hesitate to claw my way back out!"

"Ah-ha-ha! I wouldn't have it any other way!"

Suddenly, the whole world shook.

"...You will never escape. You will never leave! This false world will be your graves!"

With the last of his strength, N'nabadu was trying to collapse the dimension in on itself with everyone still inside!

"this is bad! milo!"

The two boys were shocked to see the ground rise up and over them in all directions as space-time shrank in on itself like a contracting ball.

"The dimension is shrinking!" yelled Milo. "He's trying to crush us!"

"Ha-ha-ha-ha!! The reason I created the Svapna Akasha in the first place was to eliminate you two, and now I've done it! Yippee! Yippee! Lord Rust, look at me!"

"red! hurry up and absorb the old guy's soul!"

"I'm doing it! Get ready, old man! *On-shad-brahma...*"

"*Achoo.* I'm cold."

"Hurry up, you senile old coot! Chant with me!"

"I am trying! But it is chilly without Akaboshi!"

"what am i, a pocket heater?!"

"Let's try this again. Ready?"

""On-shad-brahma-snew!""

In a blinding flash of light, the rest of Kelshinha's body disappeared, and his spirit became one with Red, causing a new tattoo to appear on her left hand. Then, without a moment's delay, the tattoo summoned a bow into Red's grip, engraved with the sutras of the Rust Lord. It was the very manifestation of the mad monk's wicked soul!

"Bisco! Milo! Let's do this!" she yelled.

"Okay!"

"all right!"

"Finishing move!"

""""Bloody Ultramonk Bow!!""""

Their bow released an arrow of pure chaos, a fusion of the pure mushrooms with the wicked Rust. Even the power of the Rust god could not save N'nabadu from it!

"Gaaaaaghh!!"

The arrow tore through his flesh without giving him a chance to regenerate.

"I-I've got to escape!"

N'nabadu flitted out of Amli's ear, and the boy's body vanished entirely. The arrow, meanwhile, kept flying until it collided with the air itself, tearing open a rift in space-time.

GRGRGRGR.

The entire world groaned, and the Earth shook! It was plain to see that the Bloody Ultramonk Bow had been the last straw for it.

"We did it!" Milo exclaimed.

"hey, look at that!"

Bisco pointed upward, toward the land suspended over them. There, the souls of the false world's inhabitants could be seen leaving their bodies and being drawn toward the rift.

"...Those are the souls he used to create this place," explained Red in a solemn tone. "They're going back where they belong."

Despite the chaos unfolding all around them, the trio stood and watched the spirits depart. All of a sudden, a glowing Amli appeared before them and addressed Red.

"Sister..."

"Amli!!"

"I knew you would free my soul eventually. I can feel many others breaking free of the Rust god's dominion and passing on in peace."

"...I see."

"how about you, amli? you able to pass on in peace?"

"Oh my! How positively adorable!"

The moment Bisco poked his nose into the conversation, Amli shot him a gentle smile.

"You must be big brother Bisco. I must say, I'm awfully envious of your world's Amli."

"i'm only cute because i got turned like this. normally, i'm over twice as big as you!"

"No you're not!" chided Milo.

"yeah, but he doesn't need to know that!"

"Tee-hee! It's good to see you two get on as well in your world as you do in mine!"

Red gazed at Amli and at the two boys, and she wasn't sure what to say. She felt a kind of relief that didn't seem like her own, and when she noticed a single tear rolling down her cheek, she quickly wiped it away.

"Amli," she said. "You don't have to worry about a thing. I *will* defeat the Rust god. You have my word."

"Sister..."

Seeing the determination in Red's eyes, Amli felt one last lingering regret.

"Do not be so hard on yourself," he said. *"The only thing I worry about is the well-being of your mind. Revenge can be a powerful ally, but it can just as well burn a hole in your heart. Believe in the power of love, not hate."*

"But...you're all dead."

Red returned only a lonely, defeated smile that tugged at the heart-strings of both Amli and the two boys standing nearby.

"There's no one left to love me."

"Listen to me. You are loved. But love is not only something you receive."

"What...?"

"The love you need, Sister...

Amli reached out a rapidly fading arm to Red. Their fingers just managed to touch.

"...is right beside you. Where it's always been..."

"What are you saying? I can't hear you!"

Red felt like Amli was trying to impart something very important to her and tried to catch up to her before she disappeared entirely.

"Wait! Don't go! Amli!"

"Watch out, Red!"

Milo grabbed her and leaped aside moments before a falling chunk of one of the towers crashed into the ground. By the time Red climbed to her feet and looked back at the spot, Amli's soul was nowhere to be seen.

"Amli..."

Perhaps she already knew the things Amli had been trying to say. But every time she tried to think of them, her tattoos burned, and the fear of opposing those vengeful souls eclipsed all hope of ever understanding.

"...It's not possible. Not for me..."

"Red, snap out of it!" cried Milo. "The Svapna Akasha is collapsing! We need to find a way back to our world, and fast!"

"*look at that!*" yelled Bisco, pointing a pudgy mushroom paw. *"there's a great big hole in the sky! can't we just jump through that?"*

Indeed, where Bisco was pointing was a tunnel through space that looked an awful lot like the one that had brought them here, and which shone invitingly.

"It's the Akasha Tripper!" said Red. "Tirol and Pawoo must have made it!"

"Let's go, Red! It won't last!"

"All right!"

The two dimensions were separated by a sea of subspace, and without a lifeline, the three would be left drifting. Tirol's portal was their only way home.

"hold on tight, milo. don't drop me!"

"I won't..."

Then Bisco, Milo, and Red used a King Trumpet to spring up toward the portal—but just before they reached it...

"You...shall...never...leave!"

"Huh?!"

...a furious voice rattled the skies above Izumo. Milo felt something latch on to his leg. It was the hand of the souls destined not to pass on but to instead vanish along with the fabricated world. They had combined...to create the Flesh Goddess the Second!

""Milo!!""

Red held on tight to the rim of the portal with one hand and gripped Milo's hand in the other.

"Hyuk, hyuk, hyuk!"

Standing atop the head of the amalgam of souls was what appeared to be the Flamebound High Priestess, Kyurumon.

"N'nabadu!" Red snarled. "You're still here!!"

The fly bellowed in Kyurumon's strong, proud voice. *"Oh, silly Red. You really thought you could kill me that easily? As long as I have vessels, I cannot be defeated! Now, time to close this little exit of yours. Do it, Flesh Goddess!!"*

"U...uh-oh!!"

The people making up the golem started chanting, and the portal began to close. Bisco clutched Milo's head in fright.

"*those guys are prayin' away the way out!*" he said.

"That's because this is a technique that counteracts the Akasha Tripper! Now you'll get what you deserve, fools! Hyuk, hyuk, hyuk!"

"Milo!! Shake them free! You gotta come, quick!"

"I can't. If we don't stop them chanting, the tunnel will close while we're still in it!"

"we don't have time to stop them! the tunnel's closin' right now!"

But while Bisco was protesting, Milo picked him off his head and brought him in front of his face. After staring into his eyes for a few moments, he threw him toward Red.

"whoa?!"

"Red! I'll protect the tunnel! Take Bisco and go on without me!!"

"Huh?!" Red caught Bisco and looked back at Milo in shock, desperate to dissuade him from sharing this world's fate. "You're crazy! Are you tryin' to die alone?!"

"Of course not. When I die, I'll be sure to take you with me!"

That's a scary way of puttin' it...

"We haven't seen the Rust god here yet, and that worries me." Milo's eyes glittered with determination, and the mantra cube shone brightly in his hand. "He might have already launched an attack on our world while we were away! That's why you have to go back! Work together and defend our home!"

"got it. you won't keep us waiting, will you?"

"Of course not!"

"Bisco! You can't let him—!"

"*milo says he'll catch up to us, so he will,*" said Bisco, with stark disregard for the life-or-death struggle about to unfold. He burrowed into Red's hair and knocked her on the scalp. *"we trust each other completely; that's the way we do things. let's go, red! everyone's waiting for us over there!*

Red stared at Milo's sweet, smiling face for a moment, then nodded.

"...Okay, got it!!"

She released Milo's hand and slipped away into the subspace tunnel.

"We'll see you on the other side, Milo!"

"Yeah!"

"Wh-what?! You're abandoning your partner to die!"

No one was more surprised by this drastic decision than N'nabadu, who was so shocked that he commanded the Flesh Goddess to drop Milo and to focus solely on closing the portal.

"*I mustn't let those two get back to the light world!*" he snarled.

"won/ul/viviki/snew..."

"Uh-oh!!"

"Rest in peace, spirits!"

N'nabadu quickly learned why he shouldn't have taken his eyes off Milo for an instant! But by that time, the glimmering mantra ax was already in his hands.

"You're lost! Let me guide you to the light!"

"Stop it!! Do you really think a weakling like you can harm my creation?! Oh no, I've got to get out of here!!"

* * *

"President's Axe: Last Rite!!"

Ker-rashhh!!

Milo's emerald mantra weapon came crashing down over the golem's head, slicing the aberration in two and bringing solace to all the trapped souls within. They stood up out of the golem's corpse, their sins redeemed, before vanishing into thin air.

"Aaaagh!! No, stop! Stay here! I promised to give those souls back to Lord Rust!"

Having escaped Kyurumon's body at the last instant, N'nabadu looked on in horror at what Milo had done. Desperately and in vain, he flew after the departing souls, trying to claw them back, but Kyurumon's soul flicked him away, and he went tumbling into the rift in space and disappeared.

"I did it!!"

Milo had ensured the stability of the subspace tunnel, but its entrance had already closed. Milo was thinking of Bisco and Red and wishing for their safe arrival on the other side, when suddenly, he placed his chin in his palm and turned his attention to a matter he should have considered a little bit earlier.

"So how am I going to get back?"

Milo's thinking had gone something along the lines of "*I'm smart, I'm sure I'll figure something out*," and now that the time had come, he was drawing a blank. Milo found it usually paid to be optimistic, but this time the wells of his fortune had run dry.

"This is bad! I can't leave Bisco by himself; just think of what he'll teach Sugar! I need to find another way home, or else…!"

But just as Milo was racking his brains over it, one of the passing souls engulfed him, wreathing him in a pale glow. Milo wondered what was happening, and then a mysterious voice called out to him, calm and gentle.

"Use my power, Milo."

"Wh-who are you?!"

"I've been waiting for this moment for so long."

It was a voice Milo had never heard before, yet it sounded more familiar to him than any other, and strangely reassuring. As if guided by the voice, the cube in his palm began to spin.

"These are the secrets of the cosmos that I discovered. They are in your hands now."

"...Blue!!"

Milo recognized the nature of the spirit whispering to him—it could be none other than Twinshroom Blue, Milo's alter ego from a parallel world!

"Milo. You will be granted a power beyond anyone's wildest dreams."

Milo felt Blue's wishes enter the cube, and suddenly it began sucking in all the ghosts in the vicinity, concentrating them into a ball of rainbow light!

"Use it to look after Bisco in my stead!!"

The light burst open, and a new world began to form around Milo and Blue, replacing the crumbling ruins of Izumo. A blinding flash of light ensued, after which Milo found himself floating in subspace, amid a cloud of stardust. Then slowly but surely, the nebula began forming together...

* * *

"Wh-wh-whaat?! My Svapna Akasha!!"

Meanwhile, a single fly tumbled through the space between dimensions, through a field of shooting stars, flapping his wings for dear life. He bore the scars of battle on his tiny back, but his compound eyes still burned with the flames of vengeance.

"He's recycling my fabricated world into something new! I never knew Milo Nekoyanagi had this kind of—no, it's her!*"*

N'nabadu searched the catalogs of his mind and swore under his breath.

"Twinshroom Blue! Her soul came with me and was waiting for her

chance! Which means that world must contain a secret that will aid the Mushroom Keepers!"

The subspace that once housed a replica Izumo now swirled like a shimmering galaxy, ready to birth a new fabricated world. He considered leaving Milo alone and going after Red instead, but somehow, he couldn't shake his doubts.

"Whatever Blue's planning, it's sure to be important! I'll show her who's the real *reality-rewriter around here!"*

And with that, N'nabadu made up his mind to follow Milo. He flapped his wings and set off into the heart of the new galaxy.

INTERMISSION

Mmm…mmgh…

…Hwah?!

Was I…dreaming?

Oh my! In the dream, Mr. Bisco was my big sister, I had died and turned into a ghost, and Father was there! It was…startlingly plausible!

But wait! Does that mean…?!

Mirror! Where's the mirror?!

…

No! However can this be?

In the dream, I was tall and handsome enough to make any supermodel blush.

And now I've turned back into a short-haired shrimp!!

Waaah! It's not fair!

CHAPTER 10

"Whoa!!"

"What's wrong, Tirol?!"

The readings on the subspace monitor suddenly changed, indicating that the encroaching Svapna Akasha had just disappeared. When it became clear that space-time had returned to normal, Tirol let out a jubilant cheer.

"The Svapna Akasha has been annihilated! No traces left in subspace!" she cried.

"What does that mean?!"

"It means they did it! Milo and Akaboshi saved the world!" Tirol slapped Pawoo on the back, the both of them seated alongside each other in the cockpit of the Banryou Tetsujin. "They got rid of that fake world that was tryin' to overwrite ours! Now none of us are disappearin' no more!"

"That's good…!"

Pawoo was sitting cross-legged, steadily supplying the giant robot with power. She let out a sigh of relief at the thought of the two boys' victory.

"Ain't that nice? Your li'l bro and your man'll be back here in no time!"

"I was not worried for them. I knew they would win."

"Liar! You could barely concentrate, you were panickin' so much!"

"I was not. My beloved Bisco has reason to return home, too—a beautiful, chaste wife such as myself. Oh, Bisco, what would you like first: dinner, or meditation, or…?"

But just as Pawoo was getting lost in her daydream world, Tirol prodded the soles of her feet, and she screamed, leaped into the air, and began rubbing her legs.

"I—I suppose we can stop the meditation here, right, Tirol? I'm getting pins and needles…"

"Not yet. We have to keep the tunnel open until those three get back. Now, get on your knees and let's get some enlightenment in here!"

"Waaah!"

Tirol was starting to enjoy bossing Pawoo around for a change, when suddenly a blaring alarm was delivered directly into her ears via her headset.

"Pickin' up a high-speed object travelin' through hyperspace!" she said, her expression turning grim.

"They must be back already! Let's open the portal!" Pawoo said.

"All right! On my mark!"

"""Launch:Akasha:Returner!!"""

The Banryou Tetsujin resumed making signs with its eight hands, and the very air shook before opening a portal through which the triumphant trio would surely return…

However…

"…?"

Pawoo felt a strange sense of unease at the approaching energy signature. At first, it tickled the back of her mind, but it quickly grew into a spine-tingling dread that caused her eyes to shoot open.

"Tirol!" she yelled. "We've got to close the portal! It's not them!!"

"What?!"

"Terminate:Akasha:Tripper!"

Without time to convince Tirol, Pawoo swiftly closed the interdimensional gate by herself—but not before allowing a single arm and leg to pop through, holding the portal open a crack.

"""What?!"""

With almost no regard for the crushing pressure Pawoo was exerting, the figure—a young boy, it seemed—leisurely glanced around at the new world in which he had arrived.

"So this is the light world… It's so…beautiful."

"That ain't Akaboshi—it's some kid! Who is he?!"

"Don't be fooled by his appearance!" An inescapable anger crept into Pawoo's voice, even as the fear caused her to tremble. "That is the Rust god himself! A wicked god, enemy of all life on the planet, come to bring ruin to our world as he did to his own!!"

"Why do you deny me?" asked Rust, tilting his head and looking down upon the Banryou Tetsujin. "Welcome me. Worship me. For I am the one who can make all your wishes come true!"

"Who would ever bow down to you?!" Tirol bellowed, but the moment she locked eyes with the image of Lord Rust on her monitor, a plethora of gold coins materialized in the cockpit, drowning her in riches.

"W-waargh!! M-money!!"

"Bow down, humans."

He had sniffed out Tirol's wish just by looking at her, and with only a thought, he had produced a fountain of treasures that could last Tirol several lifetimes.

"Whoaaa! Pure profit!!"

Tirol leaped into the sea of gold, eyes glittering as she swam backstroke through it.

"Tirol! Get it together!" Pawoo yelled. "What would your grandfather think?!"

At her voice, Tirol snapped back to her senses. With an impressive amount of willpower by Tirol's standards, she managed to tear herself away from the gold pile.

"Damn you! Don't make fun of me like that!"

"Oh?"

Rust was startled by this development and peered at Tirol with great interest.

"Do not lie, child. I saw into your mind. You desire great riches."

"Of course I do! But I wanna earn them on my own merits! There's no point in a wish that some other chump can grant!"

"Well said, Tirol!" Pawoo gave a proud nod, as if she were Tirol's own parent (despite being several years her junior). "Now, put back that gold bar you snuck into your pocket, and I'll pretend I didn't see anything."

"D-dammit..."

Pawoo was quite wise to the girl's thieving habits. Cursing the ex-vigilante's vigilance, Tirol tossed the stolen gold bar away.

The Rust god, meanwhile, looked on with interest, and a slight curve traced his otherwise expressionless lips.

"...No point, you say, in a wish that can be granted? To think even one of you powerless humans would possess a soul so pure..."

"Look out, Pawoo! He's coming!"

"Roger that!"

"You know, I think I'm going to enjoy taking over this dimension!" said Rust, raising a finger. As he did, the nail of that finger peeled off and became a tiny cogwheel that flew toward the pair.

"Wh-what's that?" cried Tirol in puzzlement.

"Watch out! It's dangerous!!" yelled Pawoo, snatching Tirol in her arm and heaving them both out of the cockpit. Behind them, the cockpit burst into flames as Rust's fingernail projectile caused an earth-shattering explosion, which instantly reduced the indomitable Banryou Tetsujin to scrap!

"""Whaat?!"""

The whole phenomenon looked strangely reminiscent of Bisco's mushroom arrows. Once Rust's cogwheel fingernail penetrated the Tetsujin's armor, it birthed many more, which tore apart the metal from the inside out.

"How?! That was Banryouji's ultimate weapon!"

"This is the power of the Rust god!!"

Pawoo's hair fluttered as she landed, and she turned toward the wreckage of the Banryou Tetsujin and picked out one of its arms to use in place of her staff. She gave it a warm-up spin in her hands, then called back to Tirol.

"Tirol, call for backup!"

"I've sent out a distress signal! We gotta get outta—! Pawoo, don't tell me you're gonna…?!"

"I must hold him off here, or else our world is doomed," Pawoo yelled. "As a mother, I have a duty to secure a future for my children! Get yourself to a safe place, Tirol!"

"Quit talkin' like that!"

Tirol shook her head to dispel the fear crawling over her, then picked up Banryouji's intelligence-enhancing invention, Mr. Brain, and put it back on her head.

"I'll help ya out," she said. "Together, we'll finish this fast!"

"Tirol!!"

"If the world ends, my life's savings'll be worthless," said Tirol, preparing a City Maker technique for Rust, who was floating, arms crossed, in the sky. "The Rust god was never born in our world. That's 'cause we don't need him! So don't be scared! We'll show that freak what common people can do!"

"Mhm!"

"Proud human," Rust spoke, his voice thick with glee. "I cannot wait until you lie broken and begging for mercy at my feet."

"Shut it, you sadistic brat!"

"If you admire our pride so greatly," said Pawoo, "then allow us to demonstrate it! Behold! The majesty of human life!"

"Launch:City:Train!!"

Tirol pressed her palms to the ground, and the earth cracked open to reveal a Yamanote Line train, traveling at top speed! It burst into the air, coiling like a snake, then, without further hesitation, went straight for the boy-sized god!

However…

"I have already seen this."

…all Rust did in response was raise his arm, and a spinning cog-wheel materialized before him. The Yamanote Line train rammed it head-on, tearing it into left and right halves, leaving Lord Rust utterly unharmed.

"Do not bore me," the god muttered.

"If excitement is what you want…"

"…then we're happy to oblige!"

"Hmm."

The second voice came from overhead, and Rust jerked his neck upward to see Pawoo bearing down on him, her staff raised, having ridden on the back of the Yamanote Line train.

"Let's go! **Boot:City:Translation!**"

Tirol's spell caused the tattered pieces of the train to re-form and join with Pawoo's staff, turning it into a miniature replica of the Tokyo Tower.

"Do it, Pawoo!"

"*Ultimate Staff Strike!!*"

Pawoo shot toward him, a streak of black hair almost unrecognizably swift! With all her might, and with the fate of the world at stake, she swung her Tokyo Tower staff down on Rust's head.

"Staff of the City: Snakebite!!"

The black snake's jaws closed down with a heaven-rattling roar! Enhanced by her sense of motherly duty, Pawoo's Snakebite technique delivered a powerful swing toward Rust's neck. The god raised a spinning cogwheel to defend, but…

"…!"

Crashhh!

Pawoo's Tokyo Tower staff should have shattered to pieces upon Rust's cogwheel shield, but instead it sliced clean through his shoulder, severing the god's arm!

"…Oh?"

"Take this!!"

The true nature of Pawoo's Snakebite technique was a two-step combination attack, faster than the eye could follow, which used the recoil of the first strike to attack an opponent in their unguarded opposite flank. The damage sustained in the first attack made it impossible for Rust to dodge the second, and…

Crashhh!!

…it reduced the god's body to scrap metal!

That got him!!

Pawoo felt she had delivered the killing blow, even before she saw his body scattered to the four winds. Humanity's proud soul had triumphed over the wicked schemes of a sadistic god.

Pawoo turned to face Tirol, still on the ground, and beamed. But Tirol's face was stricken with worry.

"Pawoo! Watch out!"

"Huh?"

"It's not over! He's—"

But Tirol never finished her sentence. Behind her back, Rust's remains re-formed, and a single hand tightened around Pawoo's throat and drove her into the ground.

Kroom!

"Gah!!"

"Pawoo!!"

"That was impressive."

Rust appeared in the cloud of dust thrown up on impact, and his metal neck cracked. Tiny parts flew to him, swiftly reassembling his missing body.

"That…can't be!"

"Must you be so easily surprised? How could a human ever defeat a god?"

"I thought I…killed you!"

"You did."

Rust stared at the citified staff in Pawoo's hands, then with just a gentle squeeze of his hand, he crushed it to dust.

"And I was born again."

"B-born…again?"

"I am the Rust god. Every soul I consume grants me another chance at life," said Rust matter-of-factly. He peered into Pawoo's quivering eyes, impressed by the depths of her mental fortitude. "Still," he said, "I cannot deny you have slain me once. You may consider yourself a god-slayer if you wish."

"Waaah!! Pawoo!!"

Tirol scuttled over and grabbed Pawoo's scruff, dragging her away. Rust simply watched them go, showing no particular interest in pursuing.

"Cough! Cough! Wh-what just happened…?"

"Are you okay?!"

Astonishingly, Pawoo seemed to have weathered Rust's blow admirably, and her life was not in danger. That was not to say it had left her unscathed, but the damage to her spirit had been greater still. For the first time, she had glimpsed the true nature of their immortal foe.

"He can be killed," Pawoo muttered, "but what is the point when death holds no meaning for him? He's on another level to us mere mortals!"

"There's no point blowin' bits off him!" said Tirol, the despair creeping into her voice as she sat Pawoo up and cradled her head in her arms. "As long as he's got souls in his belly, he can go on regeneratin' as many times as he likes. How are we supposed to beat someone like that?!"

"Perhaps it would be wiser to give up now," said Rust, as though it didn't matter to him one way or another. He could have killed the pair where they stood at any moment up to now. The only reason they were still alive was because the god enjoyed toying with their minds.

"All I did was break a single one of your weapons," he said. "Aren't you Mushroom Keepers fond of saying things like, *'We'll think of something; we always do'*?"

"H-he's playin' with us!!"

How many Mushroom Keepers had met their fates at Rust's hand after uttering those exact words? It was painful to think about. From the way Rust spoke, it was obvious he saw humanity only as a plaything, meant to keep him amused.

"We can't beat him by ourselves, Pawoo! Let's get outta here!"

"...We can't both escape!"

Pawoo took a deep breath, then rose to her feet, determination flickering in her eyes, and pulled another length of steel from the Tetsujin's corpse.

"You were always happy to listen to me go on and on about my son, my husband, or my brother," she said. "I was always grateful for that. I'm happy you're my friend, Tirol."

"W-wait, whaddaya mean by that?!" stammered Tirol, reaching out a hand.

"Go, Tirol!" Pawoo batted it away. "Live on in my stead!!"

Then she bounced into the air, aiming an all-or-nothing blow at the unruffled Rust.

"Hi-yaaah!!"

"Hmm."

Rust didn't even unfold his arms to deliver a devastating kick into the pit of Pawoo's stomach. Pawoo bent over in agony, while the Rust god followed up with a heel drop onto her exposed back.

"Gahh..."

"You have grown sluggish all of a sudden," he remarked, lifting her chin with his toes. "Have you given up already? Are you ready to abandon your husband and child and devote your body and soul to me?"

"Never...!!"

Pawoo suddenly leaped into the air to deliver a surprise follow-up! But Rust caught her staff in his teeth and swung her into the ground.

"Ghahh..."

"You are quite stubborn. But that is precisely what I enjoy... All of you crack in the end. It is only a matter of time."

Then came the Rust god's consecutive attacks, designed to shatter Pawoo's spirit.

"Gah!!"

"Guhh..."

"Aaaaghhh!!"

* * *

Pawoo was beaten black-and-blue. Her stout constitution was a curse, for if she had passed out, at least she wouldn't have had to endure the pain any longer.

I've got to get away! There ain't nothin' I can do for her!

Tirol was frozen stock-still in place.

Why ain't my legs obeyin' me? I've always cut my losses and run when I had the chance! I gotta run, or she'll die for nothin'!

Tears filled her eyes as she struck her unwilling legs with her hands. Her lip bled where she bit it, which dribbled down her quivering jaw.

"Someone...someone help her!" she screamed. "She's my friend! I'll give you all my money, my life's savings! I'll give ya everythin' I have, just... Just don't let her die!!"

T...Ti...rol...

"Oh? She hasn't run away yet."

Rust halted his punishment and looked over at the voice. Then a grin crept across his face as he got an idea. He pointed one arm and its cogwheels at the helpless girl.

"You know, I've just thought of a way your soul might be broken," he said.

"What? ...No, don't!"

"Oh? Will you bow to me?"

"I'll do it! I'll bow to you! I'll do anything you say, just don't—!"

"Then do as I say and be quiet. Watch as I grind that girl into dust."

Pawoo had stayed strong through all the violent torture, but at this, all the blood drained from her face, leaving only a mask of horror. Seeing that, Rust finally smiled. He prepared his cogwheels, powerful enough to level a mountain, aimed them cruelly at Tirol, and fired.

"Tirol! No!!" Pawoo screamed, when suddenly, out of the corner of her eye, she spotted a rainbow light.

What's that?!

"Flying Fungus!!"

The rainbow shot toward them, leaving a trail of spores, and landed like a meteor between Tirol and the oncoming attack!

That's...the light of Ultrafaith energy!!

"Mushy Magic Pole! Eight Dragons: Samsara Strike!!"

Clang!!

The rainbow-clad figure swung their staff like a baseball bat, striking the cogwheel and repelling it!

"?!?!"

Rust was not expecting to see his signature weapon reflected back at him, and he stared in mild surprise, making no attempt to dodge. Before long, the high-speed projectile collided with him, sending him flying into the side of a nearby mountain and flattening it in a cloud of dust and rubble.

"Home run!" the figure yelled, striking a proud pose. "Sugar Akaboshi, annual salary one hundred trillion sols!"

"Sugar!!"

"S...Sugar..."

The world's strongest seven-year-old and mushroom deity showed up at the last minute to save Tirol's life! The jellyfish slumped to the ground as her knees turned to jelly, while Pawoo totally forgot her injuries and bounded over to give her stepdaughter a big hug.

"You saved us!"

"I got your distress signal, but I didn't know where you were!" explained Sugar, displaying her homemade mushroom radio receiver (the inner workings of which were quite indecipherable). "But I heard Auntie Tirol's voice and came right over..." She patted the shell-shocked girl. "...and I made it just in time!"

"Auntie...? Please don't call me that," Tirol whined.

"You said you'd give up all your money to save Pawoo!" Sugar smiled sweetly in loving awe at Tirol's devotion. "I can feel the wishes of the pure of heart through my Mushy Magic Pole! So that home run was just as much yours as it was mine!"

"Huh..."

"So a deal's a deal! Hand over all your dough!"

"Huh?!"

"Ha-ha-ha! Juuust kidding!"

"...She's just like her idiotic parents!"

Tirol seethed, while Sugar went over and ran her hands over Pawoo's injuries. With a single touch, the rainbowshroom spores enveloped them, and in the blink of an eye, her wounds were completely healed. Back at full health, Pawoo hugged Tirol, then turned to face Sugar.

"We need to open the subspace tunnel to let Bisco, Milo, and Red back," she explained. "I hate to ask this of my niece, but..."

"Don't be shy!" Sugar beamed. "Sugar is the whole world's mother! It's my duty to protect all living things!"

And as if that were the end of it, she began summoning up rainbow-colored spores. Tirol and Pawoo watched as, before their eyes, Sugar conjured up a large mushroom motorcycle.

"Use this and get to somewhere safe!" she urged.

"Mm. Thank you, Sugar!"

"Run away if it gets too dangerous, ya hear?!"

Pawoo revved the throttle, and the mushroom motorbike spewed spores in place of exhaust fumes, before carrying its two riders far over the horizon.

"You worry too much," muttered Sugar, watching them go. Then, suddenly, she spun around.

"Mushy Magic Pole!!"

Dozens of cogweels rained down out of the sky, but Sugar beat them all aside with her mystical staff. After she parried every last one of them, all the giant gears rose out of the ground and returned toward their master.

"What are you?"

Rust floated dauntlessly in the air, as though he had never been harmed at all.

"You interrupted me at the zenith of my efforts. The moment I was to see a pure soul break."

"Do you thrive on mocking the sanctity of life, evil god?" asked Sugar, a divine being in a little girl's body, as she rose upon her Flying Fungus to meet Rust's eye. "Every living being upon this Earth is my own dear child. Do you want to face the wrath of a mother whose children come under attack?"

"You...are not human, are you?"

Rust spotted a spark of the divine deep within the young girl's pupils, and his expression turned grave.

"I am Lord Rust, the god of wishes. And you?"

"I'm Sugar! The mushroom god!"

Sugar waved her magic pole and pointed it squarely between the wicked god's eyes.

"I lead all life on Earth down the golden road of prosperity!"

Sugar struck a domineering pose before Rust—the pride of being tasked with her charge along with the determination needed to protect it.

Sugar? The mushroom god?

Rust recalled the child who'd slept in his arms.

I see. So she's the one...

"There's no wish I can't grant with Ultrafaith! So let's see who's better at it, you or me!"

"You are the one of which the fly spoke. The only being who poses a threat to my existence."

The sole fear of a god who could not be defeated through battle. Rust had never fought a fellow divinity before, and it was unclear what would happen if his wish-granting powers were to collide with Sugar's Ultrafaith.

"Is this...fear?"

But there was another feeling he felt as well. The joy of finding a means by which his eternal boredom might at last be relieved!

"Perhaps...," he said, "I might lose. The chances are one in a billion, maybe, but I might lose. When did I last feel like this? Perhaps never."

"Let's do this! Mushy Magic Pooole!!"

"Come, then!"

Clanggg!

Staff and cogwheels collided, and a ferocious grin appeared on Rust's face!

"You will learn to fear me, girl. You will fear for your life!"

"That's fine by me!!"

A god of ruin and a god of growth. A new chapter in Earth's history was about to be written, with the path of its future hanging in the balance!

11

The ferocious blizzard brought a biting wind that stung Bisco's eyelids.

"ugh..."

He awoke to find himself in some kind of red, spiky bush...and only upon fully sobering did he notice it was Red's hair. He was still in a mushroom body, and once he realized that, he crawled his way toward her forehead.

"red! you okay? we made it!"

"..."

"but where are we now?...whoa!"

Bisco looked up to the sky and was shocked by what he saw. Instead of a sky, an infinite darkness spread out in all directions, populated only by shooting stars. It was the tube-shaped universe Bisco had seen before when traveling through the subspace tunnel. In other words, this snowy land must have been somewhere on the way back to the light world—even Bisco could understand that.

"Something must have happened in your world," said Red. "They closed the gate, and now we can't get back."

"you mean...we're stranded here?!"

"No. We've been given a bridge," said Red, her breath condensing on the air as she hiked undaunted through the packed snow.

"*by who?*" Bisco asked. Then he noticed something strange. *"hey! where did all your tattoos go?"*

"To the bridge. They're what we're walking on right now."

"what?!"

Shocked, Bisco looked down at the long path on which Red trod. Indeed, it seemed to have been made from Red's inkings, for Bisco could see their patterns mingling together. Its sheer, icy surface was the only matter that seemed to exist in the whole space.

"If we just...follow this..."

"then we can get back to our world!"

Although there was no indication where it would lead, the pair believed. All they could do was trust those who had made it for them, so Red trudged on through the snow and ice, until...

"wah!"

She face-planted in the snow, and Bisco went flying. She had been uncharacteristically clumsy and tripped over a hardened block of ice.

"are you okay, red?!"

"Be quiet..."

"your lips are blue—you're freezin'! of course! without your tattoos to heat you up..."

Red's tattoos would have made short work of any cold in the past, but without them, she was just an ordinary girl.

"what'll we do? is there any way i can help? just say the word!"

"Shut up!!"

Red hauled herself upright once more. It wasn't just the cold that was getting to her. She seemed both physically and mentally exhausted, unable to bear her burdens for a moment longer.

...I can't die... Not here... I'll be betraying...them all...

She turned her vacant eyes on Bisco, picked him up in her hand, and peered at him, examining the spark of life that still dwelled within his pupils.

If I just... If I just eat him...

"eat me, red!"

"!!"

"i hate to admit it, but i'm no use to you like this. but if I'm a tattoo, i can help you!"

"...You idiot. Do you even understand what it is you're saying? If you die, what about Milo? What about Sugar?!"

"you'll look after them! isn't that what we promised?"

The miniature being before Red's eyes bellowed those words with such conviction that she wasn't sure how to respond.

"if we don't do something, we'll both die! you can still walk, so i'll give my life to you!"

"..."

"hurry up, or we'll both freeze to death!"

"Heh!"

Their conversation appeared to lighten Red up a little, and she stuffed Bisco back into her hair and resumed walking.

"All right," she said. "If things get bad enough, I'll eat you. But even I've got a right to choose what I put in my belly."

"what?! what's that supposed to mean?!"

"I don't want to upset my stomach, that's all."

"hey!!"

Bisco threw a fit in anger, but looking once more at Red, it was clear her stamina was running out. Her breath was pure white, with the glow of the Rust-Eater spores nowhere to be seen.

"hmm... i got it!"

Bisco thumped his palm and immediately put his idea into motion. He strained his whole body, and soon the Rust-Eater spores began floating out of him, and steam rose off him like off a kettle. Having heated himself up, he promptly dived down the back of Red's neck.

"Owww! That burns!!"

"i'm gonna be your pocket heater. where's your heart again?"

"The same place it is on anyone!"

"if you say so."

Bisco slipped between Red's breasts in an attempt to keep her warm. It felt weird at first, but as the blood returned to her extremities, Red felt her sanity returning.

"You didn't have to do that..."

"i guess i'm still useful for somethin' after all."

Bisco tried to sound unruffled, but his voice was shaking. It was clear the heat generation required significant effort.

"let's go!" he said.

"..."

"what's the holdup? let's get a move on!"

"Hah! Don't order me around, squirt."

With her strength returning, Red was free to joke around again. She gave Bisco a playful poke.

"gwagh!"

"Ah-ha-ha-ha..."

And with that, she steeled her resolve once more and pressed on through the snow.

12

"...Mr. Nekoyanagi. Mr. Nekoyanagi?"

Milo slowly came to his senses and opened his sleepy eyes to find he was standing in a lecture hall opposite a sea of eager students. For a moment, he blinked in surprise, unable to process what was happening.

"What's the matter, Mr. Nekoyanagi? Continue with your presentation; it was fascinating."

At the professor's urging, Milo finally remembered where he was—he was in a university classroom.

"R-right!" he stammered. "Right, yes! *Practical Applications of Apollo Particles*. Let's continue."

Somehow, Milo had managed to fall asleep in the middle of presenting his thesis. He cleared his throat, straightened his back, and pointed at the diagram projected on the wall behind him.

"Many structural problems have been identified when it comes to the Apollo Particles," he explained, "but we saw what they could do just recently at the Tokyo World Fair with the successful demonstration of the Tetsujin Mark I robot. That demonstration proved that these particles could be just what the world needs to solve the energy crisis. However"—Milo looked at his assistant, who put up the next slide—"many people still see Apollo Particles as a potential danger. They suggest that a critical mass could lead to the creation of an artificial intelligence that will seek to control humanity."

"And what does that mean?"

"Well, to put it dramatically," said Milo, "they are worried the Apollo Particles could birth a god of wishes bent on enslaving the human race."

Murmurs of astonishment rippled through the students in the crowd. There wasn't an educated mind in all the land who hadn't wondered how these new wish-fulfilling particles might shape the society of tomorrow. It was the buzzword of the century.

"The Apollo Particles are brimming with untapped potential, including the potential to change our society for the worse. But with the Earth's resources running dry, we owe it to future generations to boldly take the first step into wielding these particles for humankind's benefit. That is all."

Milo bowed.

"Wonderful!"

The judging professors nodded at one another.

"What a deep dive! That really cuts to the heart of the pros and cons of this miracle energy," one said.

"Trust Mr. Nekoyanagi to tackle the hard questions!" commented another.

"I have no qualms in handing out a passing grade. You other students could all learn something from Mr. Nekoyanagi here!"

Milo gave his best customer-pleasing smile and returned to his seat amid waves of applause, but a nagging feeling gnawed at the back of his mind. How did he manage to fall asleep at the podium? And had he been dreaming? If he was, Milo couldn't remember a thing about it now.

"Well then, I believe that was the last of today's presentations."

"Such a good crop of students this year around."

"All of you who are presenting next week, remember to submit any slides to the assistant two days in advance. Class is dismissed."

With their required class thus over, the students stood up and filed out of the classroom. Milo began putting away his things, still thinking about earlier, when Bisco struck up a conversation from the adjacent seat.

"Good work up there, Milo!" he said. "All that *future of humanity* jazz made my head spin. I didn't know you spent your time thinkin' about that kind of stuff."

"I don't," Milo replied. "I just picked a topic to please the professors. Our university is at the forefront of Apollo Particle research, after all."

"So you lied."

"Lying is the secret to getting ahead in society," said Milo with a wink. "Come to think of it, your presentation's next week, right? Are you ready?"

"Whaddaya mean, *ready*?" replied Bisco, scratching his head awkwardly and then looking around and lowering his voice, before whispering, "You already wrote the whole thing for me. What else do you want me to do?"

"What if someone asks you a question? You need to know how to answer! You've got to study those materials until you know them as well as if you'd written them yourself!"

"Then why *didn't* I just write them myself...?"

"Because I promised I'd help you, Bisco. You'd better come over to my place so we can rehearse!"

Milo got so lost in conversation with Bisco that he completely forgot about the strange feeling from earlier. He linked arms with his best friend, and the two of them left the lecture hall together.

Only one more academic year remained at the New Tokyo Life Science Institute. Milo had met this boy, Bisco Akaboshi, shortly after enrolling, and the two had become fast friends. So much so, in fact, that Milo had taken it upon himself to ensure Bisco's successful graduation by any means necessary.

"Hey, Bisco?" he asked, his voice bounding with energy, as the pair crossed through the courtyard. "Have you tried this month's new flavor at Baskin-Robbins yet?"

"You got one heck of a sweet tooth. I wouldn't be caught dead goin' in there by myself."

"Then go with me! My favorite is a double scoop with cookies and cream and almond fudge! Pawoo likes matcha and azuki—"

Milo turned to face Bisco, when suddenly, from overhead…

"Bisco, watch out!"

"Huh?!"

Milo grabbed Bisco by the arm and pulled, just in time to save him from a rain of beakers that fell from an upper-floor window of the university building. The pair were unharmed, but the beakers shattered, spilling their contents all over the road. As soon as the concentrated sulfuric acid within made contact with the concrete, it fizzled violently, eating the road surface away!

"Oww…," groaned Bisco, rubbing his head. "What was that for?"

"W-we just almost…"

"Oh dear!" came a voice from above. "Sorry! Are you two okay?"

An older student leaned out the window and rubbed his head.

"We were doing an experiment, and my hand slipped. Sorry about that!"

"That was serious!" Milo yelled. "You almost got us both—"

"Ah-ha-ha! Try and be a bit more careful, dude!"

"…Huh?!"

The pair's brush with death was surprising enough, but Bisco's reaction to it stunned Milo even more. He was acting as though the clumsy upperclassman had dropped nothing more dangerous than a paper cup of water.

"Let's go, Milo. What's up?"

"Uh…er…um…"

All of a sudden, Milo couldn't remember why he had been so angry. The sight of steam rising off the ground nagged at his mind somewhat, but Milo attempted to push past it.

Y-yeah, that's not that weird. That sort of thing happens all the time…

"Hello there, Nekoyanagi!"

As Milo was attempting to get his thoughts back in order, an older gentleman in a lab coat called out to him.

"You've come at just the right time," the man said. "I'm carrying out an experiment with Apollo Particle beams, and I'd love a bright young student like you to assist me with it."

"P-Professor Inabado…"

"Feast your eyes on this particle cannon that my lab invented."

Professor Inabado presented what looked like a weapon that he was carrying in both hands and braced it against his shoulder. From his description, Milo guessed it must have been some kind of rifle that fired Apollo Particles.

"Watch this," Inabado said. "With just one shot, I can—"

"Wh-what are you doing, Professor?!"

Milo's face twisted in horror. For downrange of where Inabado was aiming the cannon were several students acting as targets!

"Fire in the hole! Blam! Blam!"

Inabado pulled the trigger, and a concentrated beam of energy skewered the students' hearts, killing them instantly. The ground was littered with the bodies of other students, and yet everyone except Milo was acting as though this were all perfectly normal.

"Did you see that?!" Inabado howled. "Just one shot, and they're all dead! Ha-ha-ha!"

"Wh-what have you done?!"

"What's gotten into you, Milo?" asked Bisco, shooting him an odd look. Milo started to protest but couldn't find any words to explain what was so wrong about the situation.

"Inabado's always doin' these kinds of experiments," said Bisco. "Looks like this time the invention worked for once! But who's gonna help with your research if you kill off all your grad students, eh? There's an old man for you, never thinkin' about the future! Har-har!"

The whole conversation was unsettling to hear, as though everyone's morals had been clouded in thick fog. Milo racked his brains, but he couldn't get to the bottom of why he felt this way.

"Ha-ha-ha-ha… Oh, would you look at that! All my test subjects have died!"

"Told ya, Prof. You gotta use your head a bit more."

"Oh, what am I going to do…? Oh! I know!"

Inabado got a big grin on his face and peered through his spectacles at Milo.

"Won't *you* help me out, Nekoyanagi?"

"What?!"

"Any upstanding student of this school would be delighted to help out with a fellow's experiment, wouldn't they?"

"I—I guess so, but…"

"I think Milo's comin' down with somethin', Prof. I'll help you out instead."

"No!! No, I'll do it!"

Bisco's words finally spurred Milo into action, and he pushed Bisco aside, his mind still unable to properly process what was happening.

"I'll…be…your…target…Professor…Inabado…"

"Veeery gooood."

Inabado licked his lips, racked the rifle, and pointed it once more at Milo.

"I'll make sure you get your class credits in the next life," he said. "Here we go. Three, two, one…"

S-something's weird, I'm sure of it! But I have to protect Bisco first!

"Fi—"

"Launch:Life:Maker!!"

A clear, beautiful voice rang across the courtyard, singing a life-colored hymn! Sprouts burst out of the ground at Milo's feet, before erupting into an enormous tree that stopped the particle beam in its tracks!

Someone saved me?!

"Grr! Who dares interrupt the experiment?!"

"The Apollo Particles are the particles of possibility. They are meant to amplify humanity's potential for life."

A confident voice drew Milo's attention, and when he spun around, he saw a woman standing there, with long sapphire hair, the same color as his own. She combed a hand through it, then strode over toward the professor. As she passed Milo, she shot him a coy wink.

"I-it's you!!" Milo stammered.

"To think you'd stoop to using these particles to take away human lives…"

The woman stood before Milo, her lab coat fluttering in the wind, wearing a defiant smile.

"Don't you think that's a breach of etiquette, Professor Inabado?"

"Domino!!"

It was Milo's very own ancestor, Domino Nekoyanagi! Though his mind was still hazy, he knew for certain that she was a figure he could trust.

"Milo!" she said. "You got even cuter while I was away!"

"Why are you…? How…?"

"I asked Blue!" Domino answered, and her sky-blue nails flickered with the power of her intellect. "Don't worry, your ancestors will show you the way!"

"Well, if it isn't Dean Domino!"

Inabado seemed frustrated at being foiled just before eliminating Milo. He loaded another shot into his particle cannon, while sending Domino a nasty glare.

"I thought you were busy with research. Here to hit on the students, are you?"

"You shouldn't judge people by appearances, Professor Inabado. I'm only interested in my husband these days."

"Then what's with that scandalous skirt you're wearing? How are our fine students supposed to concentrate when you're walking around distracting them?"

"A textbook example of sexual harassment. You're on etiquette violation number two."

"Don't talk to me about etiquette, you bitch!"

All of a sudden, Inabado began to transform, his skin and clothes tearing apart to reveal a three-meter giant fly!

"Those students are my target practice! Don't get in the way, unless you want to be squashed!"

"What an astonishing lack of respect for the student body. That's etiquette violation number three!"

Domino summoned her power, and the whole campus shook as if about to explode!

"You are not Professor Inabado," she said. "You are just a wicked illusion! By the power vested in me as dean, I order to you resign!"

"Stay out of my waaay!"

"Intellect, engage!"

As one of the two progenitors of the Rust, Domino's ancestral power was overwhelming!

"Overgrow:Life:Maker!!"

The life-accelerating power of her technique caused a tree to shoot up out of the ground and entangle Inabado. The boughs tightened in on him, crushing his bones.

"Gaaaaghh!!"

W-wow!

"What's happening…?"

Milo turned to Bisco, and his face froze. Although he had been eerily quiet throughout all the disasters and atrocities so far, Bisco suddenly looked furious at Domino's actions.

"How did she escape my restructuring? How was she able to team up with Nekoyanagi?"

"B…Bisco…?"

Bisco suddenly broke into a sprint, picking up the particle cannon that had fallen onto the ground. He aimed it squarely at Domino, who had just finished disposing of the rogue professor.

"This is *my* world!" he roared. "You can't just come in and do what you want!"

"This is Blue's world," retorted Domino. "It doesn't belong to you!"

"Die!"

"Launch:Life:Reflect!"

Bisco fired a beam at Domino, but it bounced harmlessly off a coded shield made of leaves. The reflected beam hit Bisco in the chest, skewering him and causing him to cough up blood.

"Bisco!!"

"Milo! Stay away from him! He's—"

"No! Bisco! Bisco!! I'll save you, keep calm!!"

"Oh dear…"

Domino scratched her head and clicked her fingers, and a long, thin tree branch extended from her fingertips. She walked over to Milo and stuck a wooden digit into his ear.

"Ow!"

"Stay still," she muttered. "Where are you…? Over here…? Or maybe over here…?"

"D-Domino…that…hurts…"

"Aha! Found you, you little stinker!!"

Domino extracted what she was looking for, and it tumbled out of Milo's ear.

"Eeeeeee!!"

It was none other than the Rust god's obsequious servant, N'nabadu.

"Whaa?!"

"D-dammit! How did you know I was here?!"

This institute of learning belonged to the world Blue had created. However, N'nabadu had managed to hijack that world and restructure it to meet his own malicious aims. With no hope of facing Milo on his own merits, N'nabadu hoped he could use the world to eliminate him in his place, and he would have gotten away with it if it weren't for Domino's timely entrance.

"What is Blue planning? What is the point of this Svapna Akasha?!"

"You really think we'll tell you that?" retorted Domino, pulling the dazed and starry-eyed Milo to her side. "Blue trusted me to keep Milo safe from you, and that's exactly what I'll do. Don't think you're getting out of here alive!"

"G-grr!"

Fuming, N'nabadu nonetheless realized his opponents had the upper hand, and he took off on tattered wings in an attempt to flee.

"Get him! **Life:Whip!**"

Domino's nails glowed blue once more, and a whip of flowers appeared in her hand to cut off N'nabadu's escape.

"Grr! I cannot die in a place like this!"

N'nabadu's mad desperation allowed him to dodge the blows, before opening a tiny rift in space-time and slipping into it.

"Tch. He got away…!"

Domino scowled, but she felt a strange power at work keeping N'nabadu safe. How could such a powerless fly escape death on so many separate occasions?

Meanwhile, Milo slowly came to his senses.

"Wh-where am I?!"

At long last, he saw the true nature of his reality. What had previously appeared as a college campus now lay in ruins, and the figures of Inabado and Bisco were revealed to be simple mannequins of Rust. Without N'nabadu's interference, the world had returned to how it was supposed to look all along.

"Th-that wasn't Bisco? …I knew it! I knew something wasn't right!!"

"Oh? And why's that?"

"Because he actually listened to me, he didn't say anything snarky, and he didn't lash out at anyone! I'm so stupid!! How could I have ever thought Bisco was such a Goody Two-Shoes?!"

"Ah-ha-ha-ha-ha! That's so funny!"

Domino vigorously slapped Milo's back. He looked up at her with teary eyes but felt the warmth of her palm.

"…But I'm glad you're here," he said. "At least you're real."

"Blue injected me into the world directly and asked me to come find you. I came in such a hurry… Do you think I need to redo my makeup?"

"Who cares?! Besides, you're pretty enough without it!"

"I know. Hey, let's get a selfie together! Say, 'test tubes'!"

Was she always like this?!

"Blue wanted you to know something. I'm here to show you the truth."

"Whoa! And just like that, you're serious!"

Domino dropped her girlish demeanor and shoved her smartphone into her pocket.

"Apollo created the Soul Absorption Program to store the citizens of Tokyo," she said. "Milo, you should be able to use that power yourself now."

"The Soul Absorption Program?!"

"Yes. It's the same power that Red uses."

Domino turned to Milo and took his hand.

"Apollo is looking after it in one of the research rooms. Let's go, Milo!"

"Domino! We might be attacked again! I'll go by myself!"

"You must be joking!"

Domino thumped her chest with pride and flicked Milo playfully on the forehead.

"I'm the one who started all this, and you're just a college student! Why don't you listen to your elders for a change?"

13

"Nooooo!! Actagawaaaaa!!"

Those were the final words out of Red's mouth before Rust's cogwheel attack shattered the giant crab's carapace to pieces. Actagawa gave one final look toward her mistress as the light threatened to leave her eyes for good.

"Bisco!" cried Blue from Red's arms. "Hurry! Use the Soul Absorption technique!"

"But… But…!"

"Now!! Do you want Actagawa's sacrifice to be in vain?!"

"Aaaaaarghhh!!!"

With a scream more of terror than of courage, Red thrust out her arms and prepared to use her power on her beloved friend. Actagawa reached out a claw, and as soon as the tips of their digits touched, there was a bright flash of jade-green light, and the giant crab dissolved into particles. The glowing balls of light rearranged themselves in Red's hands, transforming into a giant bow, made of the same material as Actagawa's shell.

"Wh-what the…?"

"It's the *Heavencrab Bow*, Bisco! Actagawa made it for you out of her own soul!"

"I see," said Rust, looking a little miffed that his meal was usurped right before his eyes. "So you can also devour souls and make their power your own."

Rust sensed that the weapon in Red's hands brimmed with the life force of all the fallen Mushroom Keepers who had come before her, and the thought unnerved him.

...Just what is that bow?

"Lord Rust! Please be careful!" came the voice of N'nabadu, circling around his master's ears. *"The weapon they call the* Heavencrab Bow *is highly dangerous! Just one shot from that thing contains the power of a hundred million souls!"*

"What would happen if it hit me?"

"You would die one hundred million times over, my lord!" The distress in the fly's voice was plain to hear. *"That means you would lose precisely one hundred million of your stored souls! And if you have no more to lose, you will perish!"*

All this was to say that the *Heavencrab Bow* was an exceedingly effective weapon against the Rust god, and one whose threat he could not ignore.

"Now, Bisco! Fire the *Heavencrab Bow* and end this!"

"Urgh..."

"Bisco!"

"Grghhh!!"

However, as devastating as the bow was to its target, the demands on its wielder were just as great. Even Red, the strongest being on the planet, struggled to pull the bowstring taut. Her tattoos flared crimson, burning her skin, granting her unparalleled strength. Blue widened her eyes in shock at the scent of her partner's searing flesh.

"C'mon, *Heavencrab Bow*! I'm begging you... Listen to me...!"

Bisco can't go any farther! If she fires a shot like this, the Rust god will just dodge!

Meanwhile, N'nabadu noticed Red's distress and looked over curiously. *"Oh my! Look at that, my lord!"* he said. *"It looks like Red is having trouble even firing the bow! You must have frightened her into submission already! See how her hands shake! She shall never hit you like that! Why don't you fire one of your magnificent cogwheels and end her pathetic misery, hmm?"*

"You want me to kill her?" answered Rust, frowning. "Before she swears eternal fealty to me?"

"B-but, my lord, if you don't, she might—"

"Silence. I don't want to. I want to hear her spirit break."

"*Th-this stupid child!!*" cursed N'nabadu under his breath. The Rust god clearly failed to grasp the matter at hand. The concept of a permanent death was completely foreign to him, almost as though he were so supremely blessed in the physical aspect that his mental side had not fully matured.

"Do something about this, fly," he ordered.

"Please be reasonable, my lord! I am only thinking of your safety!"

"Be quiet, or else I shall crush you."

"B-but, my lord—!"

As the two villains quarreled, an opening was created!

"Take this! Mantra Whip!!"

Blue seized that opening like a bolt of lightning, lashing her mystical weapon and entangling the Rust god so that he couldn't move! Under normal circumstances, Rust could have dodged such an attack easily, but his argument with N'nabadu distracted him just long enough for Blue to finally get the drop on him.

"Lord Rust!"

"Well, well..."

"It'll be much easier for the *Heavencrab Bow* to hit a stationary target!" cried Blue in triumph. Her whip bound Rust so tightly, he couldn't even spin his cogwheels. Despite her battered face, Blue's eyes still shone like stars, and she began channeling more mantra energy into her weapon.

"That'll teach you to disrespect the power of humanity," she said. "Face it, you've lost!"

"You...insolent...girl..."

Rust's emotionless face twisted with fury. Freeing one arm, he grabbed the whip and pulled, bringing Blue flying through the air toward him.

"Aaaghh!"

He caught her in a stranglehold, threatening her to undo the spell. "Get this off me," he yelled. "Get this off me!!"

By the time Red was ready to fire, she looked up, only to be faced with Blue's plight. "Milo!! Let go of the whip!"

But she wouldn't! "Bisco! Fire the *Heavencrab Bow* and we win!"

"Don't you dare, Red! Fire now, and your friend will die, too! Do you really want to lose the very last of your allies?!"

"Rgghhh...!"

Red clenched her jaw, quaking in her boots, bitter tears rolling down her cheeks.

"Do it, Bisco!!" Blue yelled. "This is the moment everyone gave their lives for! You have to do it! Make a future for Sugar to live on in!"

"Don't you dare, Red!"

"Fire! Please, Red! Shoot!!"

"Urgh... Ughh... Aaaaaaaahhh!"

Red screamed as if her heart were being torn in two, and she released the bowstring. The arrow moved swiftly as lightning, clad in an auroral glow.

My death...it approaches.

"Lord Ruuust!!"

Fwoom!!

...

......

The arrow passed several millimeters to the side of its target, tearing off the Rust god's arm and sailing into a distant mountainside, where it exploded, leaving an enormous crater.

* * *

...She... She...missed?

If it had hit, the *Heavencrab Bow* would have erased the Rust god from existence. But right at the critical moment, Red's aim had faltered...or perhaps, it had been on purpose.

I missed.
Even though everyone was counting on me...
Even though everyone's hopes were riding on me!

A look of despair came over Red's face. Then there was a thud, and the body of her partner landed at her feet.

That was it. It was for her. That was why Red had missed. So that Blue would live. So that Red could be by her side forever.

"...Milo?"

"..."

There was no response. Just an endless stream of blood that poured from Blue's lips, so vigorously that there seemed to be no stopping it, and it stained Red's clothes from the waist down.

Red's stunned silence was broken by the Rust god's voice. In his hands, he held a crimson mass of flesh—Blue's heart. "Why didn't you hit?" he asked. "This one would have died either way. Can your meager brain not even handle that one simple calculation?"

He splattered the heart in his grip.

"N...n...nooooooo!!"

"Bis...co..."

"Milo! I'm here... I'm right here!!"

Racked with terror, Red pulled Blue close. The girl's eyeballs swiveled, following the source of Red's voice, but they failed to register her presence. Red felt an unbelievable loneliness.

"...Where, Bisco...? I don't see..."

"No... No..."

Wet with Blue's blood, Red could only weep. She couldn't come to grips with what she'd done. All she could fathom was that in a few cruel moments, her partner would breathe no more.

It was the fly's gleeful voice that shattered the silence.

"Hyuk, hyuk, hyuk! You iiimbecile!"

He danced before Red's eyes, reveling in her despair. He frolicked in the blood pooling at Red's knees, splashing lukewarm blood all over her skin.

"What was all that talk about the Heavencrab Bow*?! You'll never get another chance like that in a million billion years! All those people entrusted their souls to you, and you blew it! Ah-ha-ha-ha-ha!!"*

"Urgh... Milo..."

"Ha-ha-ha-ha! Well? Have you figured out how you're going to say sorry? Sorry to all those you disappointed? Sorry to all those whose lives you wasted?"

"Waaah! Waaaaahh!"

"She's crying! Get a load of that! Ah-ha-ha! Ah-ha-ha-ha-ha!"

"Leave it."

N'nabadu's gleeful gloating came to an abrupt end when Rust floated down to ground level, and the servile fly began buzzing around his master's ear instead. Meanwhile, Rust slowly regenerated his missing arm, meaning that the ultimate result of Red's and Blue's combined efforts was that the Rust god was no weaker than when the fight started.

"Now stand, Twinshroom Red."

"What...?"

Red turned to him. On his face was a smile of unbridled cruelty.

"This is not enough to break you, is it? Use your partner's death. Turn her life into anger and fight. Listen to the souls of the warriors that burn within you."

Red did as she was told and listened to the voices of the lost.

* * *

Destroy him.
Destroy him, Bisco.
Destroy him…

"No…"
"What?"
"I want to die," said Red in a voice about to break. "I want to be with Milo again…"
"Heh-heh-heh! Why so frail all of a sudden?!"
At last, the Rust god heard the sound of a cracking soul. A great joy welled up inside him, as though the true torture was only just beginning!
"You are the only being left in this world who can stand against me," he said. "All those fallen warriors are counting on you to finish the job. Stand. Fight. Win. For the sakes of those tattoos across your body, you must defeat me, Red!"

"No! I don't want to, I don't want to… I'm not going to!! I can't! I can't take it. I can't do it. I'm not a hero. I'm just a girl!! …Milo's going cold… Please kill me… Hurry up and kill me!!"

* * *

"you idiot!!"

Red woke up to the sensation of two small and pudgy arms striking her cheeks.

"Wah!"

"wah."

Sweating, she looked around, but nothing she saw reminded her of her dream. She was in a temporary shelter that she and Bisco had made out of a tentshroom in order to stave off the snow and ice.

Although she knew it was a dream, her heart wouldn't stop pounding. *Oh yeah*, she thought. *Blue's gone.*

Her large eyes quivered in the light of the glowshroom fire.

I remember now. Back then, I was completely broken. Tirol erased my memory, put a lid on my despair...all so I could bring myself to fight against Lord Rust.

"you should never beg for death, not even in your dreams."

"..."

"guess a ghost musta gotten into your dreams. but it'll be okay, so long as i'm around to look after you!"

Bisco hopped onto Red's shoulder, clapped his mitts around Red's cheeks, and pulled.

"so sleep easy. i'll protect you from whatever comes!"

"...Liar..."

"huh?"

"You haven't protected anyone. You *can't* protect anyone!"

Red suddenly stood up and grabbed Bisco from her shoulder, throwing him into the fireplace. Bisco leaped out, aflame, with a shriek of agony, and rolled around in the snow to cool off.

"*what's the big idea?!*" he yelled. *"what's your beef with me?!"*

"I want to kill you already," Red shot back. "How can you love everyone so much? You don't deserve to be loved when you haven't done anything to earn it!"

"what?! take that back, right now, or else!"

"I hate you! I just... Why are you still alive...?"

Then, for some reason Bisco couldn't fathom, Red began to cry. He held back the insults he wanted to shout in return and listened.

"All you're good for is killing. Killing everyone around you, and then yourself. You're just one person! Why did everyone put their trust in you? Maybe everyone would still be alive...if they didn't try to love Bisco Akaboshi..."

"what are you...?"

"It's all because they loved you. It's all your fault!"

Tears streamed down her face, rolling down her lips until it was difficult to even go on talking. It was only then that Red even seemed to realize she was crying.

"I hate you. I hate you. Why do you even exist...?"

"..."

Red broke down and sobbed, not even saying words anymore. Bisco remained motionless for a while, silent. Then he finally realized what the blizzard outside, cloaking the bridge of souls in ice, really meant.

Red's tattoos are the power entrusted to her. But they're a curse that burns her constantly. This blizzard must be what she came up with to protect herself from that heat.

"Waahhh... Waaahhh..."

Even though she looks like she's always burnin', truth is, she's been livin' in a world of ice this whole time.

Bisco looked at his alter ego once more, hugging her knees and shivering in the cold. He made up his mind and hopped atop her legs.

"Hic. Sob..."

"..."

"...Don't come near me," Red whined. "I'll bite your fucking head off."

"you're not biting anyone with frozen jaws."

"..."

"stay still."

Red felt a wave of warmth wash over her as Bisco exuded the heat-giving spores from his body. She lifted her head, and her reddened eyes met his.

"take a quick rest. i bet you've had no time for yourself, with those tattoos pushing you on, have you?"

"..."

"sounds rough to me! but i get it. i always hear jabi inside my head tellin' me off, too. but you don't have to care what dead people think."

"..."

"if you don't want to fight the rust god, then you don't gotta. let somebody else do it. you live how you wanna live."

"But then...everyone loved me for nothing..."

"who says it's gotta be for *somethin'?"*

Bisco's words lit a tiny flame in Red's eyes.

"*nobody loves another 'cause of what they'll get out of it,*" he said. *"just think of milo, pawoo, tirol, and actagawa. none of 'em love me because they want to control me. they all want me to live life how i want…and i think that's true for you, too."*

"B-but the tattoos…" Red's own words caused her to shiver with fear. "They're ordering me to succeed. It's burning me up inside! If they just want the best for me, then why is that?!"

"that's you doin' that to yourself."

"…!!"

"that voice you hear, pushin' you to win? that's your own voice. the tattoos have never been sayin' anythin' at all. they want you to be happy—those are the prayers they've given you. it's only you who sees that as a burden."

"…"

"you can still change, red. you can live your own life. i bet that's what they would want, too."

From her knees, Red looked up at Bisco. She didn't know how long she stayed in that position, neither saying anything nor moving a muscle, but in the end, she realized she had stopped shaking.

"…It's too late," she said. "Even if I could find my own life, there's no one to share it with. Milo's dead. So is Pawoo, Actagawa, Tirol… I envy you, Bisco. I know it's horrible, but I do…"

"then come live with us!" Bisco hopped merrily onto Red's knees. *"you know, here in the light world, i have another kid named salt. real smart, you'll see if you talk to him. sugar likes you, too, and i'm sure milo and pawoo wouldn't mind."*

"…It'd get confusing, having two Biscos."

"*well, i'm already doin' the work of two husbands,*" said Bisco, thinking back and shuddering at all the times the Nekoyanagi siblings dragged him around. *"really, you'd be doin' me a favor. so whaddaya say?"*

"…You're a silly man," said Red, and at long last, her lips curved into a smile. "But that sounds nice. I'd like to meet this Salt…"

"all right! welcome to the family, then!"

"Hah!"

Red flicked Bisco off her knees. Having warmed up nicely, she gave her limbs a good stretch.

"If you insist," she said. "Just you wait, though, you'll regret having me around!"

"i can't believe you did that! ...hey, look outside!"

"The blizzard..."

Until a moment ago, it had been impossible to see one step ahead, but now the wind and ice had completely stopped. Not only that, but all the piled-up snow had melted, revealing that the tattoo bridge was glowing with a warm orange light.

"*look at that color!*" said Bisco. *"it's not the bright red of mindless violence, and it's not the ice blue of self-loathing. it's the light of the sun that watches over us—the light of the rust-eater!"*

"...On-ul-brahma-snew."

Amid the streaking starlight of the subspace tunnel, Red closed her eyes and took a deep breath. When she did, the tattoos making up the bridge returned to her, carving warm orange symbols onto her skin.

It was the mark that proved she had overcome all her chaos and fear—the mark of Atman Bisco!

"whoa! wh-what's happenin' to you?!"

Red traced a gentle finger across herself. "...I feel them," she said. "The tattoos of my true self... I see, so this is how warm they were supposed to be..."

"what a crazy power. it ain't about changin' the world, like my ultrafaith—it's the infinite power of self-acceptance!"

Red kindly picked up the small red mushroom, his eyes as wide as plates, and smiled a motherly smile.

"I finally understand the mistake I was making all this time," she said. "I have you to thank for that."

"*but why did you put them back?!*" yelled Bisco, casting a helpless eye over the expanse of space around them. *"without a path, how are we gonna get back?"*

Red smiled like a goddess, then adopted a demonic grin. "Well, I was getting tired of walking!"

Her tattoos pulsed, and sunlight spores began floating around her, forming into a truly enormous weapon.

"Come to me! *Atman Sutra!*"

"*what's that?! some kind of giant crossbow?!*" cried Bisco. Then he realized how it was positioned. *"don't tell me...you're gonna fire us from that thing?!"*

"Very perceptive." Red grinned. "Can't hide anything from my own self, I guess!"

"you're crazy!! now I know how milo feels all the time!"

"And you've got me to thank for teaching you!"

Red laughed and made Bisco cling to the back of her neck before she aimed the crossbow into space and racked the string back.

"We'll break through the walls of subspace and enter the light world that way. You ready?"

"how can i ever be ready for that?! just do it!"

"If you say so. Three, two one...!"

""Fiiiiire!!""

Ka-chew!

The bolt shot out faster than light, soaring through space on its way back to Bisco's home.

14

"Watch out, Flying Fungus!"

Sugar's magic cloud whipped between the incoming cogwheels, dodging them by a hair's breadth and closing in on the Rust god. She stored up a planet's worth of power in her tiny body, and then...

"Take this!!"

...unleashed it all in one attack!

Slash!!

"Oh."

"How's that?!"

Sugar's diagonal swipe with her Mushy Magic Pole completely tore apart the Rust god from the waist down.

"Very good. You killed me twice."

"I'm not done yet!!"

Sugar immediately swung her pole for a follow-up...but the Rust god's destroyed legs re-formed in the air behind her and delivered a devastating spinning kick to her vulnerable back!

"Gagh!!"

"However..."

As the force of the hit propelled Sugar toward him, Rust ignited some sort of rocket jets from the bottom of his torso, meeting her with a fearsome tackle!

"Ghah!!"

"I still have many more souls to draw upon."

Rainbow spores dribbled from Sugar's mouth as she endured the boy god's harsh glare. The girl's attack had brought him one step closer to death, but there was still plenty of time for Rust to eliminate the source of the troublesome Ultrafaith once and for all. This battle was a true test of godhood for the both of them.

Rust frowned as Sugar painfully stood up once more. "Why do you seek to protect humanity?" he asked. "I do not wish to see a young god die in vain. Surrender the light world to me, swear eternal fealty, and you can live forever in peace and harmony."

"Shut…up!"

"Listen well, Sugar. Life is weak. Life is suffering. Humans cannot take their sorry lives; that is why they seek refuge in dreams. They would give it all up to experience just a moment of true pleasure. Money, beauty, fame…" Rust extended an arm to her. "By protecting those lives, all you are doing is prolonging the world's suffering."

"No…!"

"You force mankind to live, while I offer them a choice: to exchange their lives for what it is they truly desire. And I know all too well which one they prefer. Sugar, I implore you to see reason. We could work together. Humanity would no longer live in fear. Well?"

"The only one living in fear…is you!!"

Grimacing in pain, Sugar shot Rust her father's signature glare.

"Me? What do you mean?"

"Why do you grant people's wishes? Because you're scared of what they're capable of if you don't! Because you know that accomplishment is the only true weapon against servitude!"

"…"

"Money, beauty, fame. What's wrong with wanting those things? People are free to dream of anything! A wish is a wish, even if it never comes true!"

You dare…

"Because life's not found at the end of a dream! It's made along the road you follow to achieve it!"

Rust was taken aback by the dazzling gleam in Sugar's eyes. He had only ever seen human souls as food or playthings, and it was his first time coming face-to-face with someone who praised their worth so openly. But what irritated him more than anything was that he couldn't find one word to say in his defense.

"All you bring to this world is suffering," he said. "I suppose I have no choice but to destroy you after all."

"I'd like to see you try!!"

Sugar lunged on her magic cloud once more.

"Pathetic."

Rust stepped to the side, evading her staff and retaliating with an overhead hammer fist! The blow knocked Sugar clean out, tipping her off the Flying Fungus and sending her plummeting toward the ground.

"Time to go extinct."

Rust peered down at her plummeting form, then detached the cogwheels all over his body and hurled them after her.

Boom! Boom! Boom!

The projectiles struck Sugar one after the other, with enough force to shatter the land in two. The impact threw up a cloud of dust and rainbow spores, after which there was only silence.

"..."

The cogwheels returned to Rust, and he stroked them, folded his arms, and cracked his neck.

"She was a foolish foe, but a powerful one," he said, rubbing his growling stomach. It was a sign that many of the souls within him had been allowed to pass on as a result of Sugar's efforts—perhaps ten million of them, by the god's reckoning. Yet even that was only ten percent of his full capacity.

"I doubt I will ever experience losing so many souls at once again. I shall pay my respects and see her dying face for myself..."

Rust waited for the dust to clear, but just then...

"You'll pay for treating our boss like that!"

"...Hmm?"

"We'll get you!"

"Grr!"

"Stupid!"

...Rust felt something squishy grab ahold of his legs. When the dust cleared, he looked down to see that a whole chain of mushroom folk had manifested out of the spore cloud, connecting him to the ground below.

"What are you?"

"Bab-bam!"

"Mushrooms."

"No, monstrooms!"

The monstrooms, with their slightly dopey expressions, rubbed Rust the wrong way.

"Get your hands off me, peons."

"Uh-oh!"

"He's scawwy."

"Nope, sorry."

Then one of the mushrooms in the chain turned and called toward the ground.

"Boss, we're ready, go ahead."

"What...?"

Rust turned his eyes to the land below...and saw Sugar standing there, grinning!

"She's still alive?!"

"All right! Let's do this, everyone!!"

""""Bab-ba-ba-bam!!""""

Rust suddenly felt himself being pulled down as Sugar used the chain to swing him into the ground.

"Whoaaa..."

He tried to disassemble himself to break free, but the monstrooms were all over him, using their Ultrafaith power to foil his attempts. Although each alone was little more than a sentient mushroom, when working in combination, their purity of will was enough to overcome even Rust's miraculous power.

"L-let me go!"

"Never!"

"We're Scorpio."

"Oof."

This is not good. If this attack hits me, then...!!

"Take this! *Mushroom Chain: Fuji Avalanche!!*"

Ker-rashh!!

Combining her strength with that of the monstrooms, Sugar swung Rust into the side of the mountain, then dragged him along the jagged rocks lining its surface.

"We did it."

"You mean *I* did it."

"No, it was me!"

""""No, me!""""

"You all did great! Come back!"

Their task complete, the monstrooms all turned back into spores and disappeared inside Sugar. Using her staff as a crutch, the little god rose to her feet.

We did it...!

Sugar stared toward the base of the cliff, where Rust lay in a disorganized mess of bits and bolts. A cloud of spores lay over him as the pieces vibrated, attempting but unable to re-form.

I...I have to finish him off now...!!

Sugar set off in a sprint but quickly tripped over her own feet. What little of her energy she had not already expended to keep herself alive, she had expended on the Fuji Avalanche technique.

Just...just a little more...!

The Rust god, enemy of all life, lay just a few paces away from her in a vulnerable state. It was Sugar's chance to put a stop to his deeds once and for all, but she couldn't even move. She could only watch as slowly but surely the cogwheels reorganized, building the body of the Rust god once more.

"Well, I never."

When the god re-formed...he looked different from before.

"I never thought you would force me to *age*..."

Where there had once been a teenage boy, there now stood a

muscular young man. It was an astonishing rate of puberty by anyone's standards, but its cause was not typical. The god's shrinking reservoir of souls had forced his body to undergo a process of aging.

It was a humiliation Rust had never before experienced. A stark reminder that his days on this Earth were numbered.

"You surprised me, Sugar."

"Ur…gh…"

"I say this not out of hate but out of respect…or perhaps you could even call it gratitude."

The tall young man began walking over, his feet ringing out against the bare earth.

"Gods like us must always remain humble, lest we be toppled from our eternal thrones. How foolish I was not to realize that. But I am older now, and wiser…and it is all thanks to you, Sugar!"

Not good…!!

Still kneeling, Sugar scowled up at the approaching god.

He's grown up…and lost his arrogance!

"The container has been irreparably damaged. No matter how many souls I absorb, the young boy can never return."

Rust looked at his large hands and sighed, before turning a powerful glare upon Sugar.

"It's time to stop playing with your souls," he said.

"…"

"There must be not even a microscopic chance of anyone standing against me. I must bring about mankind's downfall in the most meticulous manner possible. There can be no room for error…no room for hope!"

"K…krh…!"

"It's a good thing I can kill you while you're still young."

Then Rust placed his fingers around Sugar's neck and lifted her off the ground. As he poured his power into his mighty grip, Sugar's bones began to break!

"Grh… Aaaaahhh!"

"There is no need for two gods in this world. Besting you shall be my final test, Sugar…!"

At the sound of her own cracking bones, Sugar finally lost consciousness, and her limbs fell limp. Rust squeezed tighter, eager to finish off his divine foe once and for all, when…

"Wait, my lord! Waaait!!"

"…?!"

A familiar buzzing reached Rust's ears, and like a speeding bullet, its bearer zipped into the unconscious Sugar's ear. Immediately, the young girl's eyes turned a deep black, and the power returned to her arms and legs.

"What are you doing, fly?!"

"Hands off!"

Sugar—or rather, N'nabadu, for it was he controlling her body—brushed Rust's hand aside with mushroom power and landed on her feet.

"Haah…haah…haah… Gulp… *Please wait, my lord. Hear me out."*

"Get out of there at once. What is the meaning of this?" asked Rust in a threatening voice, unable to untangle the fly's aims. "I was about to kill her. With you inside, you'll die as well."

"Lord Rust, you must not kill Sugar."

Even through labored breaths, N'nabadu finally managed to spit out his words at Rust's feet. For the timid fly to risk angering his master to this extent, it surely must have been something important he wanted to say.

"Sugar's body is the most powerful ingredient ever produced by all life on Earth. Let me have it, and I shall be the greatest servant you ever did see!"

"I care not. Get out of there."

"But with Sugar's power, I could even restore that aged body of yours! In fact, why stop there?! Why don't I make you a body ten times…no, a hundred times more beautiful?!"

"I said, get out, insect!!"

Finally, Lord Rust lost his temper and bellowed at N'nabadu, causing the fly to cower in fear.

"Eep!!"

He was so terrified, he had even stopped wagging his silver tongue.

"Let me tell you this in no uncertain terms, so that even your insect brain can understand it. First, this aging serves as a warning that I may never let down my guard again. I do not want it reversed. And second, a power that can amplify mine by a hundred is in and of itself a tremendous threat. It must be eliminated before all else."

"Grh...?!"

N'nabadu found this answer difficult to accept.

H-he's become more aware with age! This is not good. He always listened to me before!

"Now that I think back on our time together, fly, were you not always massaging my youthful pride to your own benefit?"

"Wh-whatever could you mean, my lord? Everything I have done, I have done for your—"

"I do not care what it is you have been planning..." Rust slowly raised his arm, and his cogwheels began charging up for a finishing blow. "...but it ends here. Your services are no longer needed."

"Y-y-you wouldn't, Lord Rust! You don't mean that! Just think of all the times I've worked tirelessly to please you! Just think of all the strategies I've hatched on your behalf, all the work I've put into achieving your grand designs! Do you have any idea how hard I've toiled?!"

"Then be grateful. Consider yourself relieved of those tiresome duties."

It seemed that, despite the fly's protests, Rust was dead set on eliminating both N'nabadu and Sugar in one fell swoop! The fly racked his brain as hard as he could, despite the shaking in his knees.

"B-but...I was so close... With Sugar in my hands, I had everything I wanted! Think, N'nabadu, think! Think of a way out!"

"Die."

"N-nooooo! ... Wait, that's it!"

On the brink of annihilation, N'nabadu struck upon the greatest idea of his life! He activated the Ultrafaith lying dormant within the girl's body and materialized her mystical weapon in his hands.

"I just thought of something, fool!!"

"?!"

"Behold, the power to transcend dimensions! ***Akasha Returner!****"*

N'nabadu stretched the Mushy Magic Pole into the air, where it tore open a hole in space-time. Subspace winds poured out of it, kicking up dust and blinding Rust's eyes.

"Trying to escape, are we?" he said. "It doesn't matter what dimension you fly to, insect. You cannot escape me."

"I'm not running away, my lord!"

"Hmm?"

"I'm bringing them here!"

N'nabadu's menial smile spread across Sugar's lips. Then, from the hole in the sky high above, something fell through, shining orange.

"What is that?! ...No, it can't be!"

"Ha-ha-ha-ha-ha!! Have you realized it yet, fool?"

Two red stars came tumbling out of subspace. Cloaked in the flames of their willpower, they each screamed:

"Rust!!"

"step away!"

""Get your hands off Sugar!!""

Nothing could have been more fortunate for N'nabadu.

"To beat an idiot, you use an idiot! Have fun killing each other, idiots!!"

15

Thuddd!!

"Gah!!"

A meteoric punch collided with Rust's jaw!

Impossible!

Never had an agent of life managed to damage Rust's immortal body, and yet the punch sent him flying, twirling, skipping like a stone, before coming to rest in a cloud of dust.

"Grr… Grrh… Grrghh…!!"

Rust propped himself up on his elbows and spluttered rust. His lower jaw was missing, and his dismembered tongue flopped out, slapping the ground with a wet thunk.

Th-this cannot be, he thought. *There is not a being in this universe that can harm me!*

"Is that what you thought?"

Through the clouds of dust where the meteor landed, there was a flutter of a glowing orange cloak. A single Mushroom Keeper slowly rose to her feet. The wind caught her cloak and flung it upward, revealing Rust's severed arm in her grip!

"Looks like you were wrong."

She leveled a confident glare at the Rust god. Atop her head, Bisco beat her brow with his pudgy arms.

"*nice one, red!*" he said. "*you really got him! the atman works!*"

…All of you.

Red looked down at the fist that had damaged the Rust god and thought of all the souls that walked with her.

I'm going to do it, everyone. Just watch.

Meanwhile, Bisco looked to and fro.

"huh? wait, where did sugar go?"

His precious daughter, the one he had been trying to protect in the first place, was nowhere to be found.

"she's gone!"

"You...are nothing but the dregs...remaining on my plate...you miserable human."

"Bisco! Rust's coming!" Red yelled, but before she had even gotten the words out...

"Sit still and wait your turn!!"

Rust ignited his rocket jets, ripping through space. The sonic boom in his wake was enough to rend the land asunder!

She just caught me by surprise, that's all. A god is far mightier than a human...especially when I am no longer my old, arrogant self.

Rust focused power into his cogwheels and prepared to retaliate, like a lion focusing all his strength on chasing down a rabbit. Like an elephant staking his life on squashing a single ant.

"Whatever meager ability you possess, I will deny you the chance to even use it!!"

Faster than the eye could blink, Rust twisted his upper body, delivering an ultra-powerful blow into Red's stomach!

Thud!!

...That must have killed her.

Feeling his cogwheels slice through Red's belly, Rust grinned, assured of his victory.

"Know your place, human."

But the next moment, something happened that caused his eyes to widen in shock.

"What?!"

Rust felt Red's abs tighten around his cogwheel punch, trapping him instead!

"This is the end, punk."

"Wh-what?!"

"Let me teach you a lesson. When you wanna punch someone you really hate..."

"L-let go..."

"You do it like *this*!!"

Thud!!

With Rust pinned helplessly in place, there was no avoiding Red's fearsome left hook!!

"Ghaaahh!!"

The force severed Rust's other shoulder, blasting his torso across the land once again. Each time he skimmed the earth, mushrooms burst to life beneath him, accelerating him onward.

Raaaaargh! This...cannot be!

As his body was filed mercilessly away by the earth, sweat dribbled down Rust's brow.

Her might is greater?! The might of a human, exceeding that of a god?!

"red!!"

That human, however, was in no condition to pursue. Rust's attack had torn open her stomach, and she spluttered blood.

"you let *him hit you? you're insane!"*

"He was faster than me. I had to slow him down somehow."

"you didn't have to go that far!"

"I'm going to win this, Bisco."

Red wiped the blood from her mouth and grinned. Seeing her eyes gleam with conviction, Bisco could find nothing more to say.

"I found out how to believe in myself. Now I can see the Bisco that everyone else loves!"

"...all right!"

Bisco put away any tactless remarks, turned to Red, and nodded. Then, summoning up his Ultrafaith energy, he placed his hands on Red's stomach.

"*i'll focus on healin' you!*" he yelled. *"so get out there and fight!"*

"You got it!"

"This…is wrong…," muttered Rust under his breath as his body slowly re-formed. Red's attack had aged him once more, and now he looked like a man in his thirties. "I am the conqueror. I am the god. I cannot be subjugated like this…"

To the Rust god, leadership was everything, and throwing souls into servitude was his only aim. He couldn't stand to be treated like those he sought to humiliate.

"…I'll pretend that didn't happen."

Rust reorganized his cogwheels onto his right arm, creating an enormous drill shape. It was a little crude for the god's aesthetic taste, but it was a small price to pay to extinguish Red with certainty.

"I shall wipe you out so thoroughly that I cannot even remember your existence."

"Quit the monologue and just do it already," said Red, jerking her chin at him. "Only reason you talk so much is 'cause you're scared, Rust."

"You will be the one quivering in your boots after this!!"

Rust reignited his rocket boosters, hurtling toward Red! Through extreme concentration, she kept her eyes trained on him and lowered her body for a counterattack.

I just have to break off the tip of that drill…

"red! look out!"

Bisco was watching the ground at Red's feet, where Rust's severed arm suddenly transformed into a cogwheel and buried itself in Red's legs, preventing her from moving.

"Grh! Dammit!"

"I gave you miserable humans everything…!"

Rust's eyes flew wide, and he prepared to deliver the final blow, aiming the drill directly at the center of the paralyzed Red's chest!

"…and I can just as easily take it away!!"

Slamm!

"Ghaah!!"

"Now dieeeee!!"

The cogwheel drill spun at high speeds, boring through Red's flesh and even her organs! Vast torrents of blood splattered everywhere, drenching both her and her attacker in red.

"Gaaaaaagh!!"

"Repent! Regret! Despair! Feel your soul being chipped away! Let me hear you beg for forgiveness, and die, Twinshroom Red!!"

"red!!"

"Grrrgh…"

"Hah-hah-hah-hah… Huh?"

"Rrrrrrggghhh!!"

There, amid a well of torment so deep that even a second in its depths would render any thinking being utterly insane…Red was thriving! She fed on the pain, her eyes gleaming with hope!! Once the drill sank deep within her chest cavity, she reached out and grabbed Rust by both shoulders.

"Now…I've…got…you…!!"

"Wh-what?! I've destroyed your heart, your lungs! How can you still move?!"

"do it, red!!"

"D-damn her!!"

Despite continually taking a lethal amount of damage, Bisco had been healing her at the same rate! But when Rust tried to aim an attack at Bisco, Red crossed her arms behind his back, pulling him in tight.

"Let's see if you can handle this, Rust…"

"S-stop…"

"Feel the hug of my soul!!"

Crkcrkcrk!!

"Gaaaaghh!"

Her awesome might eclipsed the Rust god's own! Strengthened by the Atman, her true self-realization, Red's powerful embrace caused the god's metal body to crack. A human's raw strength was about to destroy his indomitable form.

"Grrgh! Stop… Let me…go…!"

"Rrrrgghhh!!"

"Gaaaagh!!"

Red poured more and more strength into her arms, until her tattoos glowed bright with the protective light of her fallen peers. But at the same time, the cogwheel drill burrowed deeper and deeper into her vitals.

"red, we can't take much more of this!" Bisco yelled. Red's body was already saturated with the light of the rainbowshroom spores, thanks to the Ultrafaith energy he had been channeling into her. Any more and it would birth a mushroom that would tear her apart from the inside. *"you're gonna explode!"*

"Rrrghhh!!"

"Gh...gah..."

The Rust god lay on the brink of defeat...

...but if we keep this up, red's gonna...!

Red had been pushed to the brink as well. Bisco hesitated for a moment, then shook his mushroom head and made up his mind.

"goddammit!"

"Rrrghh... Huh?!"

Bisco leaped into the air and delivered into Red a devastating drop-kick! The impact tore her free from the drill but also released Rust from her grasp.

"What are you doing, Bisco?! I almost...whoa!"

Gaboom!

The ground split open where Red had been standing, and an enormous mushroom burst forth. Bisco's attack had knocked her aside in the nick of time. She coughed as the Ultrafaith sealed her chest wound, and the light of her tattoos shone brightly once more. But Red was more preoccupied with making sure Rust was dead than with her own safety.

What happened? Did I do it?

She had been able to feel Rust's godhood slipping away in her arms, she was sure of it, but she had been interrupted before the critical moment could arrive.

No, not yet! she thought. *Now, where did he go...?*

* * *

"Hrgh…hrgh… It is…hard to breathe… Hrgh…"

"Whoa!!"

As the smoke cleared, Red saw the Rust god standing before a mushroom forest…but he looked almost nothing like she remembered him. His skin was weathered and cracked, his face deep with wrinkles. He looked like an old man about to die.

"I must have…used…too many souls…," he said, wheezing. "Why… can I not breathe? Why…does it hurt so much? Why can I not heal?!"

"Rust…!!"

"Wh-what has become of me?!"

The god looked down at his arms, shrieked with fright, and began rubbing his hands across his face, but all he could feel was dry, hard skin.

"N-no… It cannot be…! Aaaarghhh!!"

He looked down in horror at his own body, which was no longer that of a beautiful young boy, but of an aged and withered man. Rust let out a primal scream and, with his cracked nails, clawed at his face and torso.

"No… No… It hurts! I'm old! I'm ugly! This cannot be me… I am the Rust god! I cannot possibly be so wretched and vile!"

"…"

"Nooooo!!"

Each time Rust tore at his skin, it regenerated right back. Red watched as the old man drove himself to madness, tormented by the frailty of his flesh, and her eyelashes quivered.

"That's what life is, Rust…"

She turned to face him, her heart and her eyes full of sympathetic sorrow.

"Do you understand now? The prayers and the wishes you made light of? Do you understand how important they were to us?"

"Grrrrgghhh!!"

"You learned a valuable lesson today."

Red's tattoos flared to life, and she began striding confidently toward the unstable old man. Rust collapsed to the floor, groaning and quivering in fear.

"Rest in peace, Rust."

"...must...eat..."

"Hmm?"

"I...must...eat...all the souls of the light world..."

Just then, Red spotted a glimmer of sadistic determination in his eyes.

He's still going!

"I can be young again... I can have my beauty back..."

"Give it up! It's over!"

"Khaaah!"

Red began sprinting toward him, but the aged god opened his mouth wide and unleashed a breath of rust. Still, such a weak attack was nothing to Red, and she swiped it aside with one arm.

"Your distractions won't work on me, Rust! Face your fate!"

However...

"Hee-hee... Hee-hee-hee...!"

"...No!"

When the Rust breath cleared, the old god stood tall, clasping something in one hand.

"...ugh...red...i'm sorry...!!"

"Bisco!!"

It was the glowing fungal form of Bisco Akaboshi!

"Ha-ha-ha... Your Ultrafaith, as you call it, caused me no end of trouble..."

Right now, Bisco was little more than a store of Ultrafaith energy, and if the Rust god willed it so, he could use the very same power that had saved Red's life to restore his own.

"Now it is mine! I shall make it a part of me."

"Rust! Let go of Bisco!"

"Now, why would I do that?"

Rust tore open his own chest and shoved Bisco inside!

"whoa!!"

"Ohhhh! The power!!"

Bisco's Ultrafaith began filling Rust's body! His cracked and broken limbs began repairing themselves, and his aged muscles grew.

"I feel it coursing through my veins!!"

"No!!"

"Bursting with power! Bursting!!"

As Rust howled with laughter, the cogwheels formed into a pair of wings, lifting him high into the sky. Then scores upon scores of gears materialized around him.

"The nobility of a soul? Why was I ever concerned with such a thing? All I need…is to devour as many of them as possible. Die. Die. Die, die, die! Die, you puny humans! All of you who live, die! Die! Die!!"

Boom! Boom! Boom!!

Rust fired his cogwheels into the land below, causing enormous explosions all across the island of Japan. As a dying old man, he no longer held any taste for aesthetics. Tens of thousands were wiped out in the blink of an eye, their souls joining with Rust to become fuel for his power.

"Ha-ha-ha! Still not enough! More must perish! I still hunger!"

"Come to me! *Heavencrab Bow!!*"

Upon Red's seeing the triumphant face of her tormentor, her tattoos sparkled, and as she called its name, her god-slaying weapon appeared in her hands!

"Oh? Do you mean to fire that thing?"

However.

"Can you, Twinshroom Red? You could not fire to kill your partner. How can you fire when it is your own life on the line?!"

"Krh…!"

"You cannot."

Rust pointed to Bisco, embedded in his own chest, and grinned.

"If you kill him, you really will be all alone. And you fear solitude. You feared it so much that you begged me for death to avoid it!"

Urgh…!!

"Yes, I know how weak and pathetic you really are!!"

The sweat dribbled from Red's brow and beaded on her quivering eyelashes. By firing the bow, she could put a stop to Rust's reign of terror, but Bisco's life would be forfeit.

…I can't do it.

Torment racked her troubled expression.

He's right. I am scared. I hated him at first. I wanted to devour him, and yet…!

"Ha-ha-ha-ha! Fool!"

While Red faltered with the bow, Rust aimed his cogwheels at her!

Just then…

"red! do iiiiiit!!"

…the mushroom Bisco, helplessly bound within Rust's chest, summoned up the very last of his Ultrafaith power, causing mushrooms to burst to life across Rust's wrists, binding them and forestalling his attack.

"Wh-what?!"

"Bisco!"

"*that name belongs to you now!*" yelled Bisco, using his final strength to bellow his message to Red far below. *"so use it to protect this world… the one i love! protect the people who loved me! pick up your bow, bisco!!"*

At that moment, Bisco's heartfelt plea reached the depths of Red's soul and awakened a feeling.

Love.

She felt it welling up inside her. There was no way to stop it. And now, when she looked at the form of her other self, she could feel nothing else. And just then, as if waiting for the last piece to fall into place, her tattoos flared brighter than ever before.

I see, she thought. *This is love. I love Bisco.*

* * *

The heroes living on within those marks all smiled at her. Red trembled no more. She called upon what she had found at the end of a long, bloodstained path of toil and acceptance—the power of self-love.

"Awakened Soul..."

With the string of the Atman *Ultrafaith Bow* pulled tight, she fired!

"...True Red Star Bow!!"

Ka-chew!

"What?!"

The arrow became a red streak, spiraling through the air. Slowly at first, but gradually accelerating.

"sh-she did it!"

Seeing the light of that arrow with his own eyes, Bisco let out a cry of joy.

"we've won..."

"Rrrghh! Silence!"

Rust ignited his boosters, but whichever way he weaved, the arrow remained in hot pursuit, building up speed!

"It's *following* me?!"

"*bisco akaboshi tends to overshoot his target*," said Bisco, a grin on his lips despite his approaching death.

"What?!"

"you've already been shot. better say your prayers while you still can."

"You fool! You'll die as well! You'll—"

Then the red arrow finally caught up and pierced its target!

"Aaaaaarrghhh!!"

"and so my journey finally ends, huh? fun times... sugar, salt, don't forget... daddy's always watchin' over you..."

"..."

"...huh? that's weird. why am i...?"
"Whoa!"

When Bisco opened his eyes, he got a big surprise. Not only was he completely unharmed, but the arrow had somehow turned him from a mushroom man into a healthy young man once more! Even his clothes, cloak, and goggles were back to their normal size.

"I'm back! But how?!"

Looking himself over, Bisco let out an elated cry, then felt his cloak flapping and realized he was still high up in the air.

"Whoooa! I'm falling!!"

Thud!!

"...Owww, that...didn't hurt...?"

"At least land by yourself. Do I gotta do everything around here?"

"Red!!"

Just as Bisco thought he was going to go splat against the ground, who else should step in to catch him but Twinshroom Red? Bisco blinked a few times in surprise, then looked around in confusion.

"What happened?" he cried. "And put me down already!"

"Is that any way to thank me for saving your life?"

"I thought you shot me. How come it didn't kill me? If anything, it did the exact opposite!"

"The True Red Star Bow wasn't made for winning battles," said Red calmly, letting Bisco back onto his feet. "It's a weapon of life, not of death. It speaks to the hearts of all those it touches, pushing them to go on. I took inspiration from Jabi's Great Spore God. This here's my ultimate technique."

"Huh. So that's why it turned me back to normal," pondered Bisco. Then, suddenly, he gasped. "Wait, but then what about Rust?!"

"..."

Red said nothing, but with a jerk of her chin, she indicated back where Bisco had just been. Bisco turned around, and saw...

"Whoa!!"

He couldn't believe his eyes. It was Rust, no longer an old man but miraculously restored to the form of a young boy once more!

"You idiot! What have you done?!" yelled Bisco, clinging to Red's cloak, face pale. "We almost had him! Now you've gone and put us back on square one!"

"Let go. That cloak's made of good material, you know. Better than yours."

"Is that really the biggest problem right now??"

"You really are a hopeless fool, Twinshroom Red. I suppose I should be grateful. Thanks to you, I once more possess my former youth and charisma, and I have nothing to fear."

Rust's revival had also restored his poise and eloquence, but meanwhile, Red looked unconcerned, her arms still crossed in defiance. Bisco looked at him and at her in confusion, then Rust prepared to strike.

"You showed me a fascinating dream, Red..."

He pulled his right arm back, charging up the cogwheels for a deadly attack!

"...but I'm afraid this is the real world. And in the real world, you can never defeat me!"

Then Red finally parted her crimson lips to speak.

"It was never me who was supposed to defeat you," she said.

"What??"

"Listen. Listen to the voices deep inside."

Her words were powerful, full of confidence, and with each one, Rust felt something, a burning heat rising up within him.

"I know you can feel it," said Red. "The souls within you are waking up."

"Wh-what?"

Slowly, slowly.

"Argh...something...burns...!"

The feeling worked its way out of the depths of his stomach, finally reaching his skin!

"Wh-what's...happening to me...?"

"Whoa!!"

"Aaargh! What is this?!"

Rust let out a shriek as strange patterns appeared across his flesh, as if being seared into his pure-white skin. They were the very same burning tattoos that had once been the source of Red's torment! One by one, they bubbled to the surface, scorching the Rust god alive in the process.

"It's the tattoos!" cried Bisco. "The souls inside him must have...!!"

"The Red Star Bow awakened them," Red said with confidence, her arms still crossed. "The very souls he tried to control with his wishes."

"S-stop it! Settle down!"

"This is the end."

"Know your place, lowly human souls. Do you really think you can fight back against me? I am the one who devours! *You* are only there to *be* devoured! That is the law of the world! Now watch! With just one click of my fingers... With just... Just... Grh!! Hey! Stop it! Stop it, right now! Don't you care for the wishes I've granted?! What do you hope to gain?! Doesn't the thought of going back out into the real world scare you? What do you think you can do without me?!"

Rust became more and more terrified as his skin blistered and peeled. Yet the burning heat did not stop, and soon enough, it reached the god's face!

"Ow! Ow! Aaaarghh!! Fly! Where have you gone, fly?! Do something! Do something, do something!! Aaagh! I'm dying! The humans...are killing me! Aaaaaaaaghh! Gaaaaaaaghhh!!"

Fwoosh!!

Finally, Rust burst into flames, expelling burning bits and bolts as a pillar of fire engulfed him, stretching all the way into the heavens. It was like being cast into the core of the sun itself, but Rust didn't die. Blessed by immortality, he died and was reborn, over and over again.

"Grant my wish..."

One death for every soul he had taken.

* * *

"Grant my wish…"
"Aaaarrrghhh!"
"Grant my wish."
"H-help…"
"Grant my wish."
"It burns… It buuurns!!"

"Red!" yelled Bisco as he watched the god burn. "We gotta do somethin'! He's not gonna die!"

"You want to end his misery?"

"Of course I do! The battle's over! He doesn't need to suffer!"

Red did not object to Bisco's wish. She nodded once to him, then looked back at Rust.

"In that case, all you need to do is fire the *Ultrafaith Bow*."

"The what?!"

"You heard me. Send all those souls on toward their next life, and there'll be no more fuel for the fire. That's something my bow can't do. Only a dreamer like you can handle that!"

"But without Milo, there's nothin' I can—"

"Help! Help! Somebody, heeelp!!"

"Dammit!! I can't listen to this anymore!"

Bisco gritted his teeth and called upon the last of his remaining Ultrafaith to summon up his miracle bow!

"Can you shut up already?! Come to me, *Ultrafaith Bow*!!"

The spores of the Rust-Eater responded to their master's voice, tracing out a bow-shaped arc in Bisco's hands, but…

This ain't the Ultrafaith Bow*!*

…it wasn't enough to materialize Bisco's ultimate weapon. The *Ultrafaith Bow* was a weapon to birth the impossible, crafted of his and Milo's intertwined dreams, and there was no way he could create it alone.

I need Milo, or else…!

"No, you don't."

"…!"

Bisco felt a strong hand on his arm and Red's pulse through his back, and he calmed.

"I believe you can do it on your own, Bisco."

"…"

"So believe in me. Believe in yourself."

Suddenly, Red's tattoos lit up and began channeling energy into Bisco's incomplete weapon. The power of Bisco's self-love finally allowed him to manifest it by himself!

"Whoa! It worked!!"

"I knew you had it in you."

With Red's encouraging smile at his back, Bisco drew the bowstring tight. His surprise turned into faith, and behind the windows of his eyes, the jade-green light of confidence gleamed.

"…I can do it!"

"This belongs to both of us."

""The Atman *Ultrafaith Bow*!!""

Ka-chew!!

Bisco released the radiant arrow of his self, and at the very same instant, that arrow skewered the Rust god's heart!

"Ah… That's better… So cold…"

Gaboom.

Gaboom. Gaboom.

Gaboom! Gaboom! Gaboom!!

The power of the Atman and the power of Ultrafaith, working in synergy, blew the god's body to pieces, ending his immortal reign once and for all. The souls trapped within leaked out in abundance and, as if guided by the arrow's calming light, returned to the great wheel of transmigration.

"...Rest in peace, you lot."

Bisco slowly lowered his bow, and it dissipated into spores of rainbow light.

"Hey, Bisco!"

Red slapped him on the back and guffawed loudly.

"Hah! What a gullible idiot! I didn't *really* think you could do it!"

"What?! But you said you believed in me!"

"I was lying, obviously!"

Red poked Bisco teasingly in the cheek and grinned. There was no longer any trace of anger or fear in her voice, only a proud warrior's heart.

"So what, just 'cause a pretty girl says a few nice things about you, you go all tryhard in front of everybody? How embarrassing."

"What part of you is pretty?" Bisco shot back. "You're just a big side of beef!"

"That's not a nice thing to say to a girl, shrimp."

"Pork chop!"

"Oh, now you've done it!!"

The two Biscos completely forgot the pains of their journey and began duking it out like a pair of warring tigers. However, as they wrestled, it became increasingly clear that Red's physical strength was superior, and after a few struggles, Red ended up on top, pinning Bisco down.

"Haah...haah... Ah-ha-ha! Learned your lesson yet?"

"Dammit! Let me go!!"

"..."

Then Red calmed down and peered into Bisco's eyes, jade-green, just like hers. For a moment, neither blinked. Bisco lay shrouded in her long crimson hair, and a bead of sweat dripped from the tip of her nose and onto his head.

"...You know?" she said at last. "There's something I wanna say."

"???"

"...And that is...well... ...Thanks, I guess..."

* * *

Then she began moving closer. Bisco struggled to process what was happening as her lips came perilously close, and then…

"Bzzz."

"…!!"

A high-pitched buzzing in her ears caused Red to leap to her feet. Bisco followed suit and leaped away from its source.

""N'nabadu!!"" the two of them growled.

"Oh, what a world… Alack and alas…"

The fly showed no signs of attacking. Instead, he flew between the pair, gliding unsteadily toward the fallen cinders of his master.

"My darling Lord Rust, what have they done to your beautiful face? Oh, my lord, my lord…"

N'nabadu alighted upon a scorched cogwheel and let out a pitiful cry.

"Oh, the humanityyy…"

"Your scheming ends here, fly," said Red, putting one leg forward. "I know you still have those billion souls you borrowed off Rust. Let them go, now, or you'll regret it!"

"Ohhh, Lord Rust, Lord Rust… Sob… *Ohhh… …Hyuk. Hyuk, hyuk… Hyuk, hyuk, hyuk! Kyah-ha-ha-ha-ha!! You stupid child! All those times you called me a worthless insect! Well, who's worthless now?! Look at what happens when I'm not around! Burned to cinders without a word! Ha-ha-ha-ha!!"*

""?!""

Bisco and Red were caught completely unawares. N'nabadu, the ever-loyal servant, seemed overjoyed at the death of his master, kicking around the lifeless cogwheels with cries of "Take this! Take that!"

"Wh-what the hell?!"

"Hey! That's your dead master! Show a little respect!"

N'nabadu froze. *"Master?"* he said. Then, after a pause, he chuckled. *"That was just a little set dressing. You need a charming presence to win over people's souls, so I created that doll and made it believe it was a god!"*

"You *created* Rust?!" Red was momentarily stunned, but soon her fighting spirit took over once more. "Don't make me laugh! Besides, it doesn't matter now, we've won!"

"You've won...? You really think you've won?"

N'nabadu gave his master's carcass one final kick, then flew into the air and sneered at Red.

"You don't understand, do you? I didn't just create Rust! I created—"

"Rargh!!"

But before N'nabadu could launch into his proud exposition, Red moved like a flash of lightning, hurling an arrow at him barehanded. N'nabadu attempted to flit swiftly to one side, but the arrow grazed one of his six legs, tearing it off.

"Gyaaaagh!!"

"We ain't got time to listen to your bullshit!!"

"M-my front-right leg... Arghhh... That hurt. That huuuuurt!"

"Red!!"

"Stay back, Bisco! We don't know what he's capable of. I'll handle this!"

"No, Red! Your leg! Look at your leg!!"

Red sensed something strange in the bloodcurdling quality of Bisco's voice, but before he could say anything more, Red lost her balance and pitched to one side. That was because her leg, her strong, powerful leg...had completely disintegrated into glowing particles!

"Wh-what the—?!"

There was no pain. And in any case, Red would have been able to sense if the fly had attacked her. It was just like when N'nabadu had attempted to erase Bisco from the world by creating the Svapna Akasha.

"What's happenin' to you, Red?!"

"My leg...it disappeared?!"

"*That's what you get,*" said N'nabadu, wiping beads of sweat from his brow. *"Beat the master, and the false world vanishes! You saw what happened to Kelshinha. Now the same thing's happening to you!"*

"That can't be right!"

"Yeah, how come *I* vanish if you go down?!"

"*You still don't get it, Twinshroom Red...*," said N'nabadu, grunting through the pain of his missing leg. Then he grinned. Raising a remaining limb, he tapped the side of his head.

"I created you. Not only that, but I created Twinshroom Blue and your own son, too. Your entire life is fabricated! The whole dark world is nothing but a Svapna Akasha of my own creation!!"

Bisco and Red were stunned speechless. Was the fly telling outrageous lies to stall for time? Red look down at her fading leg, then back at N'nabadu.

"Th-that can't be right!!"

Her voice was shaking.

"Are you saying my life, my dreams, my struggles, none of it was real?!"

"If you don't believe me, then just watch this!!"

With a crazed look in his eyes, N'nabadu grabbed one of his own legs and ripped it off. As he screamed in agony...

"Whoa?!"

This time, it was Red's burly right arm that disintegrated into spores and disappeared like smoke. Her eyes went wide, and she shivered in fear.

"Th-that can't... But that means...I'm...!"

"You're just an inferior copy! Another possibility in the timeline of Bisco Akaboshi! Now *do you understand?! You never stood a chance! Not even an itsy-bitsy one! Aaaaagh, god, it hurts!"*

Each time N'nabadu howled in pain, another part of Red disappeared. Bisco pulled a sour grimace, said "Dammit!" and ran over, grabbing hold of N'nabadu and channeling the healing power of the Rust-Eater spores.

"Owwww... Oh? My legs! They're growing back! Would you look at that?! Ha-ha!"

As N'nabadu's limbs returned, so did Red's arm and leg. But although her physical injuries were easily reversed, the mental trauma was harder to overcome.

"Looks like there's more to you than meets the eye," said Bisco. "Who are you, and why did you make Red's world? Where did you learn to do somethin' like that?"

"You want to know who I am?"

N'nabadu suddenly stopped laughing and turned to face Bisco head-on, a deep fire of vengeance burning behind the many-faceted windows of his compound eyes.

"You want to know? You want to know why I created an alternate timeline? You should know already, Akaboshi. You should know who I am. You created me! Use your damn brain for once, you imbecile!!"

The tiny fly disgorged such strong words of anger, it didn't seem possible! A dark aura spilled out of him and shot toward Bisco and Red.

"Whoa!!"

Bisco stepped forward and covered Red with his cloak, and the dark aura, N'nabadu's very despair, took hold of his mind and granted him a vision.

Wh-what's happening?!

"When your arrow pierced Tetsujin. When you killed Kelshinha."

Bisco saw an array of possible worlds. He saw Imihama in flames after Tetsujin's rampage. He saw all humankind united in mindless praise for the Rust Lord.

"You diverted the world off the path of ruin."

He saw the endgame of Tokyo's restoration, a completely urbanized Japan. He saw the death of humanity at the hands of the vengeful Benibishi.

"All those failed possibilities drifted in the sea of subspace..."

An epidemic of catitis that robbed humanity of their intellect. A great flood that cleansed the land of corruption.

"...finally coming together into a single fly!!"

All the visions of ruin were accompanied by sensations, smells, and pain that gripped the pair of them.

Th-that's it! That's what N'nabadu is! He's made of all the futures that me and Milo averted!

* * *

"That's right! I am everything that would have come to pass if you two had never existed! And my mission is to purge this false future the Ultrafaith created...by turning Sugar into the Mother of the Universe!!"

N'nabadu spread his wings and raised his forelegs up high, and a dimensional rift appeared over his head, from which emerged...

"""Aaaahh!!"""

...Bisco's very daughter, Sugar Akaboshi, alongside Red's infant son, the dark world Sugar, both wrapped in a deep sleep.

"""Sugar!!"""

"Both Sugars, to act as the body, along with a vast number of souls to provide nourishment... I've collected all the ingredients at last..."

N'nabadu glanced at Red and grinned.

"Thank you for taking such good care of your child, Red. Now he's in perfect condition for me to use!"

"N...no..."

Only a few moments ago, Red was fit to burst with anger, but now her face was deathly pale.

"Oh, what's wrong, Red? It's nothing to cry about. Here, why don't you put on a nice, big smile, like me! Yay!"

"Please...do what you want to me... Just don't harm my son!"

"Oh, there's no need to worry."

N'nabadu grinned.

"You never even had *a son!"*

"You bastard!"

"Oh, no you don't!!"

Clanggg!!

After seeing Red cry, Bisco's speed was unmatched. He drew his dagger and aimed an almighty swing at N'nabadu in retaliation! However...

"Haven't you been listening to a word I've been saying? If you kill me, Red dies as well! Don't you understand that?!"

Grrr! He's already usin' Sugar's power!

Though N'nabadu lacked any powers of his own, the Ultrafaith moved at his command, creating a shield that handily blocked Bisco's blow!

"Yes, that's the look, Akaboshi. It's finally time...to have my revenge! It's finally time to replace your future with my own!!"

N'nabadu focused his hate, and the black aura flung Bisco back, pinning him and Red to the ground.

"Stay right there and watch. Watch your precious daughter be reborn into a goddess!"

"Stop!!"

The waves of energy seared Bisco's flesh, but that didn't stop him from reaching out his hand!

"Sugar!!"

"O failed futures! Share with me your resentment! Let the fires of hate burn! Give me power! Give me Sugar, the Mother of the Universe!"

N'nabadu began gesturing feverishly, casting a spell, and as he moved his six arms, a vast quantity of souls poured into the infant boy Sugar.

"Behold! The egg from which a new world shall hatch!"

"N...no..."

"Now, Great Mushroom Girl! Incubate this new world!"

N'nabadu's creation floated over to Sugar, toward her belly, and as soon as the two touched, an enormous blast swept over the Earth!

Fwoosh!!

"""Whoa...!!"""

"It worked! It actually worked! It—! Agh!!"

The blast was powerful enough to strip the surface of the land. Bisco and Red were each flung hundreds of meters away.

"Urgh..."

Bisco staggered to his feet. His skin was grazed and bleeding all over. He ran to help Red up, then turned his eyes to where Sugar had just been. As the dust began to clear, he saw...

"Tremble in fear, life..."

...a vast goddess, her halo lighting up the surface of the entire planet. Within her mushroom raiment was another world, a sea of stars set against the midday sky.

"...for this is Sugar, the Mother of the Universe!"

"Sugar!!"

With each blink, her long eyelashes twinkled like stars. With each tiny breath, her lips exuded a rainbow glimmer. She was grown up now, and older than he was, but Bisco recognized in her the traces of his daughter.

"Demolish every world. Delete every dimension. End every life. And then give birth to a new world!"

"Give birth?!"

"Yes, and then..."

N'nabadu sat upon Sugar's palm, wearing a crown and a mad grin.

"I will guide this new world, as the Father of the Universe!!"

"Huh?!"

"Isn't that right, my darling?"

"Yes, dear."

For an instant, Bisco's fury surpassed all limits!! Seeing N'nabadu fawning in Sugar's arms, he forgot about his bow, sprang into the air, and shot toward him!

"Uh-oh."

N'nabadu saw the look of murder in Bisco's eyes and let out a yelp.

"H-he's coming for me! Sugar, do something!!"

"Yes, dear."

Bzoom!!

Just as Bisco's fist came within millimeters of N'nabadu...

"Grh!!"

...it was severed at the shoulder. With just a wave of her finger, the Mother of the Universe tore through Bisco's Ultrafaith-strengthened flesh like it was wet paper.

"G...gagh!!"

"Oh god, the blood!"

N'nabadu danced this way and that to avoid the blood splatters, then turned angrily to Sugar.

"What took you so long, you stupid wife?!"

"Sorry, dear."

"Su...gar...!!"

"*In any case, you see how things are,*" said N'nabadu, turning back to Bisco, who was grabbing on to his daughter for dear life with his one remaining arm. *"We're going to make a beautiful new life together. I hope we have your blessing,* Father."

"Sugar... Come back..."

Bisco's voice sparked a glimmer of recognition in Sugar's eyes.

"Let's go home...to see Milo...!"

"Dear."

"Yes, darling? You look so pretty all grown up! Kissy, kissy!"

"Who is that human?"

"*Oh my!*" cried N'nabadu in mock surprise. *"You mean to tell me you've forgotten your own dear father? Before you became the Mother of the Universe, you loved your mommy and daddy more than anything else in the world."*

"Did I...?"

Then she trained her jade-green eyes on Bisco's own, and both pairs of eyes stared into each other's, exchanging a thousand words without speaking a single one. Bisco could see his reflection in the girl's clear pupils.

"Oh, love! What a moving sight! No amount of forgetfulness can ever break that bond between a father and his daughter! ... Well? What are you waiting for, darling? Kill him."

"Yes, dear."

Bzoom!!

From the mother's fingertip came a blinding beam of light that pierced Bisco's left eye. He began falling through space, but never once did he stop looking at Sugar.

AFTERWORD

I am a man with time on his hands.

I don't drink, I don't hang out with anybody; I just wallow endlessly in peace and quiet. You may be thinking, *What an easy life*, but I implore you to think about it for a moment. How long do you think the average person would last when faced with eternal boredom?

And having time on my hands means I invariably spend it in my own company. Busy people find their attention shifting to the outside world, and they forget about themselves, but within the cage of solitude, there is only the prospect of debating philosophy with oneself for all eternity.

What a terrifying thought.

Hmm? Stop making excuses and just write the next book, you say?

You know, you can't just barge into an author's afterword and start throwing around entirely reasonable demands like that.

Anyway.

Why am I talking about free time all of a sudden? That is because talking to oneself, and in particular learning to love oneself, was the central theme of this very book.

Do you love who you are?

If I were to pose this question to Milo, I have no doubt he would respond in the affirmative almost immediately. That is because he is a narcissistic panda. However, I suspect Bisco would have a harder time formulating a response.

He probably doesn't know.

Bisco's life is like an arrow and fraught with self-sacrifice. He always tells people to live life for themselves and for no one else, but in truth, there is nothing he loves more than shedding blood, sweat, and tears for others' sakes.

What a great guy. However, it is not a mature worldview. Self-harm is not the same thing as self-sacrifice, and I think Bisco needs to learn how to truly value himself if he is to ever gain the courage to love another human being.

So I decided to intervene and to sit Bisco down opposite himself to see if the two of them (one of them?) couldn't reach some sort of mutual understanding.

And as you can all see, it went rather well. I think in the future, we will see a Bisco who has learned not to be so stoic all the time, and who can use his love for himself to deepen his relationship with Milo.

...Hmm? What future? Oh yes. As it turns out, the story is still going.

You see, I had originally intended for this volume to be the last. As for why, well, to be perfectly honest, I felt like my creativity had run dry. In fact, I rather think it ran dry around the conclusion of Volume 3, and it is only through blood, sweat, tears, and pure luck that I have made it this far.

So when I was coming to the end of this volume, I felt a wave of relief wash over me. At last, the burden of this story was lifted from my shoulders...

...and then, a flash of inspiration!

The story doesn't end here!

And so the tale continues.

You must think me irresponsible, but I'm afraid poor Shinji Cobkubo has no power over Bisco or Milo, or indeed any element of the story; I just write down what happens to them. And if they say the show must go on, then so be it. What do you expect me to do?

Sabikui Bisco is not over just yet. And I would be forever grateful if all you lovely readers would look over Bisco and Milo for just a little while longer.

Until next time,

—Shinji Cobkubo

The Rust Wind eats away at the world. A boy with a bow matches its ferocity.

SABIKUI BISCO

10

Final Volume

PROMISE

"Do partners stay together forever? Even after death?"

"Yeah."